CW01509305

Praise f
Aka, things found whilst ego-surfing

'…*plenty of action, suspense and humour and no shortage of Easter eggs and obscure references to keep you on the lookout. The final section is impossible to put down.*'
Jonathan Gilmour, review on Amazon of Go Baby Go

'*If you like Terry Pratchett read this book.*'
Meghan VP, review on Amazon for Murder Incorporated: A Film Noir Love Story

'*Great read. This book achieved its aim of sucking me in leaving me desperately craving more. I for one will be keenly awaiting his next adventure.*'
Av3n, review on Amazon for Two Days a Nightmare

'*Wow. This is most definitely a four star book. From death, tumult and chaos comes justice in a biblical sense that is up-lifting.*'
D. Register, review on Amazon for When the Man Comes Around.

'*Great example of the genre. Short, punchy and brutal. An excellent example of the genre with an undercurrent of the paranormal.*'
Ansonia, review on Amazon for When the Man Comes Around.

'*The books are really good, but could you not write something with less violence and bad language?*'
Kyle's mum

MERRILY MERRILY

THE LONGEST JOURNEY VERSION

KYLE SPENCE

1

DEDICATION

To Cure (the Andrea, not the band)

CONTENTS

.

ACKNOWLEDGMENTS

Lucy and Andy for proofreading another one, knowing that all fault and blame will be transferred onto them right here.

GENTLY DOWN THE STREAM

Evening was falling over a semi-detached house in one of those little country villages that some might call quaint, though others might say boring. It was falling elsewhere too but right now we're concerned with this one house in which little Sophie Weaver is lying in bed with a yucky tummy and runny nose.

Being sick and getting off school always seemed like a good idea when you're eight years old, when they talked about it during break time everyone seemed to forget the actual part about being sick. The dizziness was awful and there was currently a small fortress of snotty tissues building up around her bed.

And worst of awful she wasn't even going to miss any exams.

There was little to entertain during the day when you had to stay wrapped up, there were no cartoons on television just some people fighting on a stage, and some guy with mad hair looking at antiques. Sophie hated antiques, why did people pay so much for old junk when you could just go out and get new stuff that looked good?

Adults could be quite silly sometimes.

But not Daddy, he called her his Little Buttercup because of her blonde hair; he made her feel strong and protected. Daddy didn't seem to be around an awful lot lately, he had been staying away from home and wouldn't say to Sophie where he was, only that he was not far away. He had been around more often since she had gotten sick, usually when he arrived there would be hushed but not exactly nice sounding words downstairs and then Mummy would leave. Daddy would lie next to her and he would hug her, tell her that everything was going to be alright. Sophie thought that he needed to be strong because Mummy cried a lot. She spent a lot of time with Sophie, helping her and looking after her, but sometimes it felt like it was too much.

She was happy now to be tucked up in her bed with her funny green nightlight glowing in the corner next to her gently bubbling fish tank with more ruined castles in it than fish.

As she cuddled her somewhat ragged Floppsy Bunny her eyes were starting to get heavy and she could feel herself starting to drift off to sleep. She kissed Floppsy on the head and hoped that her tummy would feel better tomorrow; she was getting lonely being away from all of her friends.

Just on the edge of sleep, that moment before the dream when the world seems most real yet entirely imagined there was a thump from somewhere at the end of her bed like a toy had been knocked over or a pillow had fallen.

Sophie didn't think much of it until she heard a slightly mechanical voice say 'Whoopsie'.

"Is somebody there?"

That was a silly question to ask she thought before the words had even finished exiting her mouth, of course somebody was there, he had said 'Whoopsie'.

"Oh my," a tin face popped up at the end of the bed, "the last step is always a bit higher than you think."

A small tin man with an oversize pointed nose and a rakish tricorne hat climbed up onto her bed and sat down, crossing spindly legs that ended in oversize shoes and leaned gloved hands on his ball shaped knees. He was painted in roguish swashbuckling clothes and looked like the kind of old-fashioned clockwork toy that had been rapidly discontinued the moment that safety standards became a thing.

"You would not think that would be tiring," he wiped his brow, "but let me tell you..."

"I think I have a fever," Sophie said, unsure if this was real or a dream. It should be a dream, she was fairly certain that mechanical men didn't exist in the real world, not in any useful sense at the very least, but on the other hand she was also fairly certain that if it was a dream he should have brought ice cream, "Who, or what are you?"

"Oh right, you do not know me," he backflipped into the air like his legs were on springs, because they were, before doing a cute little curtsy, "I am Walker, knight and guardian to the Weaver. That would be you."

"Weaver is my surname, my name's Sophie."

"Yes, Ms Weaver," he did another little bow and Sophie saw a large brass key sticking out of his back, like an old windup tin soldier or something.

Crawling out of her bed sheets she touched one finger to his pointy big nose and gave a gentle push that made him fall to his backside with a cry of 'Hey, quit it.'

"You're made of metal?" She looked at her finger, his skin had felt cold and hard.

"Do not be so judgemental," he crossed his arms and his robot lips did their best impression of a trout-pout, "it is what is on the inside that counts."

"Oh, sorry," she hadn't meant to offend him, and up until this point in her life she hadn't considered that toys could be offended, in which case she probably owed a few recently balded dolls an apology, "like a soul?"

"No," he sprang from one foot to another like a hyperactive Jack Russell terrier, "clockwork. I am a Clankydoodle."

"That's not a word."

"A robot guardian," he flexed his arms like a body builder, the thin piece of the tin actually seemed to bulge, "not as impressive as my big brother though, I just cannot get the Austrian accent right."

"But why are you here," Sophie sat on her feet, "I don't need a guardian, I need medicine that doesn't taste like liquid worms."

Walker climbed up the bed to sit opposite her with his legs crossed, he smiled and pushed his hat brim back with one finger like a cowboy in one of the old movies that Mummy watched, with the guy who had a mean right hook and said 'pilgrim' a lot.

"I have been sent on this quest to protect your Lucining," he said as if it were the most obvious thing in the world.

"I don't think that's a word either," she crossed her arms, "what's a lucining supposed to be?"

"You will find out in about three seconds," he stood, Sophie watched as he came to stand beside her with his hands out and palms open.

"What-"

Her eyes became overwhelmingly heavy and she tipped forward, Walker caught her and gently laid the little eight year old Sophie back in her bed and tucked her in. He placed a hand on her forehead and felt how warm it was.

"See you soon."

*

Sophie awoke in a near darkness lit only by a constellation of fireflies and staring at what looked to be the inside of a drain pipe that had not been cleaned in a very long time. The ground beneath her was soft and spongy, like moss, and as she sat up she realised that was exactly what it was, a big mattress of dry moss.

Looking around she saw that she lay in a small cave and the scraggly bits hanging from the ceiling were actually small roots poking through from the plants above. There was a slightly brighter light created by a small purple thing glowing in the corner, like some weird kind of queen firefly or glow bug that was watching the intruder to its cave with a wary curiosity, like the way a cat looks at you when you enter your own kitchen.

"Good morning," Walker jigged happily through the cave entrance, Sophie looked past him to the starry night time sky and wondered if there was a screw loose in his clockwork. In the back of her mind a little voice said that there was something different about him, but it was currently drowned out by other priorities.

"Why am I in a cave," she was pretty certain scary stories started like this, "where did you take me?"

"The Kingdom of Trancelvania," he said with the cheery pep of someone who didn't need a morning coffee, "we are not far from the village of Cuddleton."

"And how did I-oh!"

Sophie had stood up and banged her head on the ceiling, which caused her to fall backwards onto her bum, she looked up at the roof and it was far too high for her to have hit it.

Getting onto all fours to stand she noticed that her arms had gotten a lot longer and more slender than the slightly chubby and awkward little things she remembered. As she rose the ceiling got close very quickly and she found that she had to crouch.

"I've got bigger," she said as she patted her arms, chest, and legs, then in sudden remembrance of her mum shopping for clothes she checked her bum to make sure that she wasn't massive, but it was hidden under layers of lace in a green ball gown, "what's going on? Why am I in a gown?"

"You are the Weaver," Walker shrugged with a slight whirring of gears, "you must see yourself as a princess."

"Princess?" She gave the dress a little test swish, "I didn't know I was so precious."

Sophie realised that it was not just her body that had changed but her voice too, she sounded like Mummy. As she stepped carefully out of the cave so as to not bang her head again she felt a smile spread across her face as she was able to stretch out her arms and raise her head high.

In the end Sophie couldn't help but laugh, this was wonderful, it was amazing to be able to stretch so far. She had always thought it would be scary to be so far above the ground and that big people must have being walking around with this constant dread of tipping over. Now that she was here though it all felt so natural and being small by comparison felt clumsy, and well, a little bit silly.

She fell backward into a bed of moss and kicked her feet into the air, giggling at how long her legs and arms were.

"Did that bump on the head drive you mad?"

"No," Sophie sat up with a broad smile across her now elegant adult face, "I've never been this big before, it's amazing. How did you do it?"

"I did not," Walker offered her a hand, as he pulled her up he seemed to grow in stature as well, "you did, you are the one weaving the world around you."

"I'm doing it," Sophie looked puzzled as she was able to look Walker in the eye as she had done when she was the height of an eight year old, "how?"

"I do not know," he shrugged his shoulders and then spotted her toy rabbit on the ground outside the cave, as he passed it to her he said, "you are the Weaver, I am simply your guardian."

Walker then drew a long and curved sword, the type that Sophie recognised from all the old pirate shows, a cutlass she was pretty sure they were called. He checked that the blade was sharp by slicing through a weird purple plant that looked like a carrot and deflated with a slow farting sound, and smelled just as bad.

Then as he sheathed the blade he rolled his shoulders in a way that caused his clockwork insides to click and then jumped back and forth from one foot to the other. She noticed that the key on his back had gone soft and was hanging like a rather fetching bronze cape.

"Well, I am all wound up and ready to go," Walker stretched his shoulders back and struck out his chest, "we should make a start, we have to find the bravest and strongest heroes of the land."

Sophie never noticed that the firefly that had lit the cave had changed into a small sprite who was watching on with a happy interest. When the girl left to follow the clockwork man the sprite let her light dim and she became the pixie that she was, she watched the Weaver walk off and she smiled to the twinkling stars before turning into a large owl and flying off to her next task.

"Walker," Sophie caught up with the tin man and stopped him in his tracks, she looked nervously at Floppsy Bunny in her hands as she knew that she wasn't going to like the answer to this question, "why am I here?"

"To save the Kingdom of course," he said with an oblivious smile, and Sophie felt like she needed to go to the bathroom, either to pee or be sick, it could go either way at the moment.

2

A WALK IN THE WOODS

"Hey, wait a minute," Sophie tried to keep up with Walker as he merrily strode into the dark and scary woods that surrounded their little cave like the icky hair that gathered in the plughole, "hey, would you stop whistling and talk to me for a minute."

Walker was practically skipping through the mossy ground and fallen branches whilst Sophie was struggling to keep her feet. She thought about how high heels were a bad idea for a forest trek and then with a yelp of surprise she suddenly stumbled forward.

Pulling up the hem of her dress she saw that her high heels had transformed into ugly brown hiking boots.

"Well, that's better," she said, confused as to how she was making these changes, "I guess?"

"Come along, Miss Weaver," Walker cheered as he poked his head from around a tree, "we still have a ways to go."

"Wait," Sophie ran to catch up with him, "what's all this stuff about saving the Kingdom?"

"Do you remember when I wished you a good morning?"

Walker paused and looked back at Sophie and she became very aware of the fact that she was now standing in a spooky forest at night with a total stranger. She was pretty sure that Mummy had told her not to do that.

"Yeah," she took an instinctive step back, "when does the sun rise?"

"It is a little after nine in the morning," Walker looked past the gaps in the trees to the stars above, "the sun has not risen in two days."

"What, like it slept in? How does the sun not rise?"

"Nobody knows, the light just went away," the clockwork man looked down at his oversize feet, "it has been getting colder without the sun. I was sent to find a Weaver in the hope that you can make it shine again."

"But how? I'm just a little girl," Sophie lifted her currently adult sized arms in such a way as to show off her dress, "who apparently thinks that she is a princess, I'm not an adventurer."

To her surprise the gown had become a green tunic and dashing white pantaloons, and matching brown satchel to go with her hideous brown hiking boots; something a bit more fitting for someone going on an adventure. A hooded cloak appeared on her shoulders to round off the look of dashing adventurer chic.

"Well alright then, I guess I'm an adventurer now," she really wished that she knew how she was doing this, "but let's get back to this bringing back the sun business. I did enough science in school to know that the sun doesn't go anywhere, we move around it and the planet spins to cause night and day and astrology."

"I do not know how were are to save the Kingdom per se… but I believe you can," Walker took a step forward and placed a reassuring hand on her arm, "but in case that does not work out we will need the help of someone wise and of someone strong."

"I suppose you were told all this by a kindly wizard who smokes too much and hangs around with dwarves?"

"The Oracowl of the forest came to me. I don't know if it smokes."

"Oracle you mean?"

"No, Oracowl," Walker smiled and started back on his path through the trees, "it is an owl, a really big one."

"Oh... kay," Sophie raised an eyebrow and followed the weird tin man a few steps behind, she wondered if maybe there were a few cogs missing from the adding machine in his head.

"Are birds of prey known for their sage wisdom?"

"Eagles live as far away from people as possible," Walker nimbly jumped a fallen log, "chickens are a tasty dinner. Which one would you say is smarter?"

"I wouldn't want to fight an eagle for his drumstick," Sophie said as she brushed a stray branch out of her path.

She noticed that the leaves on the trees all seemed to be fluffy clouds as if they were made from cotton candy, and felt just as sticky. Absently she tore a bit of the fluff from the nearest tree revealing some green underneath followed by a shout of 'Oi!'

Pausing by the branch Sophie saw something hairy sitting in the greenery next to a web-like hammock, she swatted the air before her as it threw a cloud of hair.

"I don't go breaking into your house," the spider said as it wove a patch over the hole, "I swear, some people think they can go around doing as they please, tearing up webs, no consideration for the hardworking arachnid."

"Ooh," Sophie said, trying not to burst into a terrified run, "sorry about that."

The spider continued to grumble about the 'Two Folk' having no respect for an honest day's labour and something about shift work. Sophie didn't know what that was but it didn't sound like fun.

Rushing after Walker she grabbed his spindly little arm and stopped him in his tracks with the determination of someone who knew that they weren't going to like the answer to the question they were about to ask.

"Walker, are all of these trees," she cast her eyes around the thousands of fluffy branches that surrounded them, "are they filled with spiders?"

"Of course, this is Spiderholme," he brushed a few of the thrown hairs from Sophie's face, "they are spinster spiders, they work in the silk factory on the edge of Cuddleton."

"Are they," she looked nervously around getting that ticklish feeling you get when you know that a spider is in the room but you aren't quite sure where it went but it must be somewhere close and it's in your hair right now, "are they dangerous?"

"Nah," he started walking again, "they can get a bit surly sometimes, but you would get in a bad mood too if you had to spend all day weaving cloth with your bum. Usually they are quite friendly."

Scratching at an imaginary spider behind her collar Sophie decided to stick next to Walker and hopefully they would get to somewhere a little less creepy a lot more quickly.

*

Far, far away from Sophie and Walker hidden in a mountain valley that would be black even in broad daylight there stood what might charitably be called a Dark Tower.

Really though the place looked like something that had been sneezed onto the planet by a passing Cosmic Horror with a bad dose of the flu, and the resultant mess had congealed into this sprawling fortress of darkness and bad vibes.

The town within its walls might once have been a lovely place but now it was home only to banshees and ghouls, and one passing internet troll who really liked the ambiance.

The buildings were empty, with tiles missing from the roofs and paint faded and flaking on their shingles, the stone walls were stained every colour on the dirt spectrum from snot to pee. Rubbish, broken parts and abandoned carts littered the streets, market stalls sat with their produce still on display but the food long since gone rotten.

It was as if one day everyone had simply vanished. Not just the residents but everyone who knew about the place and out of spite it had taken on a dark determination to ensure that no one came back.

The black tower loomed over the town like a grim and overly enthusiastic prison guard watching for the first inmate he could beat up and throw in the even worse part of the dungeon with the chains and unexplained drips. The tower stood silently watching for any movement, it was keeping a hateful eye on everything.

In places it was built in straight lines but in others it looked as though the stone had bubbled and melted to form some kind of living shell, its black foundations had twisted to wrap themselves around the outer walls of the fortress, spreading like a monstrous blob of joylessness into the valley.

The trees and grass around the fortress had turned yellow and brown like something a heavy smoker would cough up. And beyond the grass was the Cracked Vale, a fracture in reality caused by the dark tectonic forces of the fortress and a place that was the geographical equivalent of a mood ring; sunshine and happiness when it felt like it, and listening to Norwegian black metal music when it didn't. Animals no longer came near the valley and the once blue river that passed through the city and under the fortress now didn't so much run as ooze.

Once upon a time this had been a beautiful place, that people from all over the land travelled to, but since the dark came and the magic was gone it had turned to brooding and a place of despair. The nightmare had spread out like a sickness to infect everything around it.

Nobody came to the valley anymore, even its name had been taken by the veil of dread. People now only knew it as the Castle of Pandemonium, home to a Queen blinded by anger and paranoia.

*

Sophie and Walker had been tripping and stumbling through the dark forest for an uncountable time. With no daylight it was hard to tell if it was even still morning.

Aside from a few bruises from falling as she got used to her new size Sophie found that she was not getting tired in the slightest. She discovered that since big folk didn't have to waste energy on the whole growing thing they got much better miles per gallon.

A few song birds had tried to sing uncertainly, they knew it was supposed to be bright and singing was their gig but on the other hand people tended to shout rude things if they sang at night.

The birds weren't the only animals that were having a difficult time of it. A quick and sprightly fox had been seen darting between the trees like a hairy ninja only to be chased home by his vixen for being out gallivanting at this time of the day.

Walker was still humming merrily to himself as if he had not a care in the world, which was quite possible if his brain was just a bunch of cog wheels.

He still had not explained how he expected Sophie to be able to bring back the sun and what she understood so far it seemed to be a four step plan that went along the lines of:

Step 1) Find a Weaver

Step 2) Go... somewhere

Step 3) _ _ _ _ _ _ _ _ _ _

Step 4) Sunlight

It did not instill her with confidence.

He also had not explained to Sophie what being a Weaver meant beyond 'it means being a Weaver', which in the grand scheme of things was not an awful lot of help.

She couldn't shake the nagging feeling that Walker was just making this up as he went along and hoping for the best.

"Ah, here we are," he said as Sophie walked into the back of him, she hadn't noticed that he had abruptly stopped.

There was a wide gap in the forest and as she looked instinctively both ways Sophie realised that this was a cobbled street. To her right was the edge of the forest and the first of a few odd shaped houses with low walls and high thatched roofs. They looked like big versions of the little porcelain miniatures that Mummy used to buy until the infamous afternoon of the Earthquake slash Barbzilla attack. What remained all disappeared after that.

Lanterns burned along the road leading into the village and farmers ran carts of wares up and down the street to a bustling market.

"Welcome to Cuddleton."

COUNTING SHEEP

"Come on," Walker hopped merrily on his spring-loaded legs along the cobbled street, "let us get you some lunch and then we will see about finding some help for our quest."

"Is it lunchtime already?"

Sophie knew that they had been walking for a while but it didn't feel like it had been so long since she had awakened in the cave. Time really does pass quicker when you're big.

The streets of Cuddleton were a mix of grey and brown, a combination of stone and horse poo, and it smelled an awful lot like cow farts. The buildings and outhouses that lined the roads all had grey stone or whitewashed walls, none of which were taller than Sophie but extended into huge thatched roofs with high peaks.

The people that they passed did not seem to be letting the lack of sunlight get them down; they all had jolly round faces with large noses and bright rosy cheeks, even the women which was kind of odd. They went about their business carrying bundles of wheat or pushing carts of food without a care for what darkness may have befallen the Kingdom of Trancelvania.

Even Sophie knew however that crops needed sunlight to survive and she wondered if the people here had ever set aside stores of grain.

"Walker," she looked around at all the happy faces, "do these people know the trouble that they are in?"

"They are rural folk," he replied, "usually they just put their heads down and get on with it, they do not know how long the night will last."

Sophie had the frightening thought that these people were depending on her, an eight year old with a sick stomach and she was expected to save the day. She began to feel a lot smaller and the charming houses around began to have a much more 'looming' aesthetic.

"Walker," she could feel tears form in her eyes, "I don't know how to fix this, I don't know how to make this better."

A cloud of rain rolled in and the townspeople simply put their heads down and moved their goods under the shelter of market stalls and porches.

"It is ok, you just have to do what you can," he lifted a horse blanket that lay abandoned along the road and held it over Sophie's head, "that is all that anyone can ever do."

Walker ducked under the blanket himself for fear that some of his joints would start to rust.

"One more thing though," he said quietly but earnestly, "let us keep you being a Weaver as our little secret."

"Why do I get the feeling that you are going to tell me something that should have been said before we started so that I could say no?"

"There are people who will fear what you can do," he

nodded toward the rain, "and there are some who are much worse."

A crack of lightning lit the sky and a clap of thunder boomed around them causing Walker to nervously duck his head.

"Let us go to the inn until you calm down," he said, "I am very aware of the fact that I am made of metal and standing in a lightning storm. Never the twain should meet."

*

The Inn of the Counting Sheep was ringing with music and bustling with all manner of creatures the likes of which Sophie had never seen before. There were pig nosed men; hulking great creatures made of stone with moss growing out of their ears; weird jelly-like creatures that smelled faintly of strawberry and who ate by setting pieces of fruit on their head and sucking it in, which made them kind of look like walking trifles. An octopus wearing a glass diving bowl filled with water played at an old honky-tonk piano like Beethoven on several large coffees.

There was also a family of frogs, one goat, and a jolly innkeeper with a belly so large that Sophie wondered how he could reach the thick wooden counter.

And when they had opened the door the music stopped and every single one of these weird and wonderful creatures turned to regard with whatever they had that passed for eyes the girl in the door and the clockwork man. As a normal human being Sophie realised that she was probably the strangest one here.

The pause unnerved her but the silence lasted for all of three seconds before the crowd went back to their own business and the jaunty melody of the piano rang out once more.

Walker shook out the horse blanket then led the way through the bustling tables with a smile on his face, the rural folk paid them no more heed and Sophie began to feel a lot more comfortable, and maybe a bit bigger again.

She looked around the cosy room, seeing past the strange people to look at the actual inn; all old and heavy beams of dark brown timber, barrels on stands behind the counter, and a floor of grey stone, covered in sawdust. The walls were stone up to the first floor and then wood rising to the thatched roof.

A few ladies in what Sophie had heard Mummy refer to as 'racy outfits' stood around a balcony talking to some cowboys with their hats tipped and hips cocked, a negotiation of romance to which Sophie's innocent mind was oblivious.

Walker came to a quiet corner table with two stools and a lamp burning softly overhead, he pulled out one of the stools for Sophie before straightening up.

"The stew here is great," he said, "I will order some for you and I am going to ask around to see if there are any libraries or wizard towers in the local area."

"Libraries?" This sounded dull.

"We need someone wise to help us," he shrugged with a whirr of his joints, "that means book smarts. We might get lucky and find someone strong too among all the country folk."

Sophie wasn't sure what to think, other than that a clockwork man with no stomach or taste buds probably would not know if the stew was great.

As she watched the tin man skip off on his spring loaded legs Sophie wondered just how smart the funny little man could be. Cog wheels by themselves could not think and surely there could only be so many possible combinations in his pointy little head. Of course she had heard the saying 'greater than the sum of its parts', but that didn't normally apply to what was essentially a gearbox with agency.

The fact that he seemed endlessly happy unnerved her a bit, when Mummy was like that it usually meant that the doctor had given more of those pills that she hid on the top shelf of the medicine cupboard.

She had no doubt that Walker had the best of intentions but if he had no idea what had caused the sun to disappear then good intentions meant about as much as a lawyer in a submarine. Actually Daddy said they all belonged at the bottom of the sea so that was might be a bad example.

Looking about the room she did have to hold back a giggle at all the funny creatures and the quirky ways that they talked to each other and ate their food. They all seemed so happy and carefree, like a weird mix of fantastic dreams or something and it made her feel weirdly comfortable, safe even.

Whatever else there might be about this strange little town Cuddleton was a haven for all people.

And suddenly in a far corner of the room her eyes locked on a boy; he was bigger than a boy and dressed all in black with a black hood pulled over his head as he tried to hide in the shadows. Sophie had been able to catch a glance at his face: it was Billy Brand, a boy who would pick on her at school. What was he doing here?

Sophie turned away from him and pulled her own green hood up over her head, she didn't think that he had seen her and she decided that it was best that he did not.

A kindly looking lady with long floppy ears like a King

Charles Spaniel brought over a bowl of thick potato and meat stew and placed it before Sophie along with a glass of cold milk.

"There you go, dear," the innkeeper's wife said, "would you like me to get you anything else?"

"No, thank you," Sophie said, and then she stopped the lady, "actually, over in the corner there is a man in black sitting, does he come here a lot?"

"Stay away from him, dear," the innkeeper's wife looked across at Billy Brand skulking in the corner and her ears perked up, "he's one of those Shadow People, he showed up here soon after the Long Night started."

"Shadow People?"

"Purse Loyals from the desert," she said, her voice hushed, "vampires they say, banished to the wastes beyond Trancelvania and cursed. They only show up now as mercenaries, paid to fight or to commit crimes. Just keep your head down, dear, if he's here then he's looking for something and it can't be for any good."

"I'll watch myself," Sophie gave a broken smile, and feeling a bit smaller again, "thank you."

The floppy-eared innkeeper's wife had a big honest face and she smiled down at Sophie giving her a friendly pat on the shoulder before walking back to the kitchen.

Sophie leaned on her hand and tried not to think about the obnoxious boy in the corner, she reached into her satchel and stroked at Floppsy Bunny for comfort. With any luck they would be leaving soon and that brat would be left far, far behind.

Dipping a wooden spoon into the heavy bowl she helped herself to a hearty scoop of the stew and almost immediately her eyes lit up. It really was great.

A FERTILE IMAGINATION

Walker skipped in his usual joyfully oblivious way across the Town Square toward the library on the corner next to a four storey sweet shop.

The sky had cleared up and already the cobblestones were starting to dry, he knew in his cogs that this meant the Weaver was starting to feel better. He didn't know how he knew but he knew and that was enough for him. Machines either know something or they don't, they don't have the capacity for philosophy in the same way as organic things who started by asking why and ended not knowing if they knew the thing that they knew or not.

Lanterns were having their oil refilled around the market square as traders began to reopen their colourful stalls and display wares that ranged from exotic to unidentifiable. Despite its rural aesthetic Cuddleton seemed to have the same cosmopolitan offering as the back alley of a major European city at the height of the Silk Road trade.

Walker caught the attention of a random brown cow that a farmer was in the process of trading with a giant for some magic beans. Seeing a significantly brighter future with the cheerful looking robot who presumably wasn't a fan of rump steak she crept off after him on the tips of her hooves.

It was on passing the statue of Walter M Cuddle, gruff founder of the town and a man desperately in need of his namesake that Walker began to get that feeling on the back of his neck. If he'd had hairs they'd be standing but his paint went on doing the bare minimum that paint does, still, he knew that he was being followed.

Turning around he found himself nose to wet nose with a tip-toeing cow.

"Oh. Hello?"

She gave him a curious sniff, followed by an equally curious lick, and she seemed to satisfy herself that he wasn't carnivorous.

"I am afraid that I am not in need of dairy products, they are not good for the gears you see."

He tried to shoo her away but she stared back at him with big, innocent eyes and continued to chew on some cud.

Slumping his shoulders in defeat he turned and continued on his way toward the library, hearing the clop of hooves and gentle chomping behind him.

As he walked through the door to the library he was stopped by a man who was either a really old looking boy or a really young looking pensioner, it was hard to tell under the moustache and mad mop of grey hair.

"I'm sorry, sir," he barred Walker from going any further, "you'll have to leave your cow outside."

"It is not my cow," Walker tried to explain, "I think that she just likes me."

"Nevertheless I am going to have to ask you to take her

outside."

"But."

"Now, sir."

"But, but."

The librarian crossed his arms like a headmaster who just caught three boys trying to sneak into the girls' locker room, it was a look that told Walker that there was no room for negotiation.

Turning with a sense of rejection probably felt by the same boys being denied a peek at unmentionables he trudged back through the door and sat on the steps outside. The cow followed as if she found something strangely interesting about the clockwork man; she nuzzled his metal shoulder and he shooed her away with a deflated wave.

"You do not happen to know if there are any wizard towers around here?"

He looked over his shoulder and the cow chewed on her cud, staring blankly in response. Walker stared down at his feet.

"This would be easy if you were a big dog," he said, "I could just say sit and stay and you would park your bum on the ground."

"Oh cool, a Bos Taurus of the Jersey family, page 203 of Pat Cow's *A Common Agricultural and Animal Husbandry Guidance for Ye Lordly Folke of the City*," a voice said from behind him, "how did you get her to do that?"

Looking around Walker saw that the cow was sitting like a dog and looking back at him expectantly, she gave a lick of her lips.

Next to the cow stood a heavy looking book with two legs jutting from between the pages and on the front of the leather cover was a smiling yet somewhat curious face, he was looking inquisitively at Walker.

"I uh, did not know that she had done that," he stared at the big eyes of the book, "I am sorry, but you are a talking book?"

"No need to apologise, it's an accurate observation," the book stretched out a stick-like arm to pat the cow, "and you're a Clankydoodle with an omni-rotational self-winding power spring, quad gyroscopic stabilisation, and I'm guessing from your speech a two hundred and fifty six cog logic engine."

"Five hundred and twelve cog," Walker said with a sense of professional pride, "how did you know that?"

"It's my job to know things, "the book offered a spindly hand, "the name's Wikki."

"Walker," he returned the handshake and nodded over his shoulder, "what are you doing out here, surely you should be in there?"

"Oh, no, libraries are like waiting rooms, a book's place is out in the world," Wikki smiled, "I was just returning myself to spread some gossip."

"Well, if you do not have anything else to do and are looking for a new adventure I think I know someone who you should meet."

"Two days after the sun disappears and we have sudden inexplicably changing weather, I think I can guess," the book smiled, "I'd be happy to join, if nothing else it will be more interesting than the slightly greasy stories from the romance novels."

The Jersey cow watched on with mild interest, the funny metal man and the heavy brown thing seemed to be getting very excited about something. This could be fun.

*

Sophie finished up her bowl of stew and as she sipped on her milk she glanced around in the non-casual casual way that people use when they're looking around but trying not to look like they're looking around, and it's always painfully obvious that they're looking around. She was trying to see if Billy Brand was still skulking in the corner like a hungry spider.

He seemed to have disappeared, much to her relief. Billy Brand was pest enough at school without also being here in this Kingdom, though it did not surprise her that he was what the innkeeper's wife called a 'Purse Loyal'. He liked to pick on the smaller kids to look tough to the popular crowd.

How he had got here was a mystery though. The innkeeper's wife said he was one of the Shadow People, could they move between worlds the way that Sophie seemed to have done? Was Billy Brand really from Trancelvania? Whatever the case it was quite a feat for a boy who was generally regarded as going nowhere.

She didn't have any idea what a Weaver was but could it be possible that Shadow People were in some way like her, only bad? If they were like her why wouldn't they do something useful and try to help these poor people? No money in being a hero to farmers she supposed.

"Ooh," a surprised yelp came from across the inn.

Looking around Sophie saw two bushy trees sprouting on either side of the counter, their leaves glowing with a soft golden light.

"Uh-oh," Sophie said, with the realisation that she was the one making it happen, "stop. Stop."

Another golden bush sprouted under her stool and she had to bolt from her table as it began to push out into the room parting customers and furniture alike. She melted into the confused group of patrons in the centre of the inn as the trees continued to grow through the stony floor, pressing against the windows and popping them out of their frames.

"Everybody outside," the innkeeper shouted in that bellow particular to innkeepers normally heard at 2am as the golden trees pressed up against the roof causing the wooden walls to groan.

Lanterns were knocked to the ground but before the fire could catch and spread the trees as if by intention pressed against the casks of beer causing them to burst and wash away the flames.

Squeezed between one of the pig nosed men and one of the anthropomorphic boulders Sophie was carried in a tide of people as they pressed their way to the door.

In the market square outside Walker and Wikki stood rooted to the spot and stared as light shone from the branches that had pressed out through the windows of the Counting Sheep Inn. The whole building seemed to be bulging as the people rushed out.

"What the stars?"

Branches pushed their way through the thatched roof and continued to rise into the sky, as more and more pressed through the market began to grow brighter.

Squirming free from the crowd Sophie looked around until she spotted Walker standing with a book on legs and a cow. Running over to him she dared not look back as the trees continued to rise, taking the thatch from the roof entirely and the trunks twisting around one another.

"I think we should go," she said.

"Did you do this?"

"I was thinking how sad it was that these people could lose all of their crops," she looked back and saw the mighty trees grow and spread their boughs, "I was wishing there was something I could do to help. Then that happened."

The townsfolk stood in awe as daylight spread across the town from the golden leaves.

Amazingly the walls of the inn still stood, and there even looked to be ample space inside for the inn to keep doing business and to spare the family any hardship.

"You are right," Walker looked at the people, "we should go before the people start wondering how this happened."

"That's amazing, you really are a Weaver," Wikki said as they slipped away from the crowd, and Walker grimaced.

The word rang like a bell in the crowd and spread through them like the inexorable force of a tidal wave. One after another they began to look around with a mixture of excitement and awe, Weavers were as legendary as Big Foot or honest politicians.

"That was supposed to be a secret," Walker said as he began to rush Sophie away from the increasingly excited people.

"I'm sorry, you didn't tell me it was a 'secret mission' we were embarking on," Wikki jogged alongside, "you only asked me about a new adventure that was a bit hush… oh."

"I've never seen a talking book before," Sophie looked at the large volume keeping pace with them, "who are you?"

"The name's Wikki," he smiled up at her, "purveyor of fine knowledge to those in need. Technically I'm a Tome, not a Book."

"He is our wise man," Walker clarified, quietly questioning if he was wise or just knowledgeable, "book smarts at least."

"Moo," said the cow by way of introduction.

The word went out like a circus coming to town and people were appearing from every nook and doorway as the group got out of the market square and onto the main street. More and more people came to see the new dawn and the news spread that a Weaver was responsible, they soon took notice of the young woman in the green tunic with the hood pulled up trying to look inconspicuous.

"Quick," Wikki said, "think about the cow turning into an airship."

"What?"

"Moo?"

The cow had a moment of shock as she suddenly lifted into the air like she was filled with helium and flew ahead of the rest of the group. From somewhere far behind they heard a confused call of 'Hey, that's my cow'.

The cow inflated until she became a massive blimp overhead, her legs turning into ropes and her hooves came together to form what looked to be an old fashioned sail ship hanging underneath, like a galleon or pirate ship. The blimp had two bumps like horns on the front and fins on the back shaped like curled tails, the ship's prow had a cow head instead of a wooden lady on the figurehead and its name in golden letters across the stern was 'Daisy'.

As Daisy touched the ground a gangplank bounced down allowing the group to run aboard as the crowd slowed their approach, it wasn't every day that you saw dairy cattle become an effective form of air transport.

The gangplank rose back into the ship by itself and the airship lifted quickly into the sky over the stunned crowd.

As Sophie looked over the side at the gathering of people

there was first applause and then a loud cheer as in the golden glow of treelight the shadow of Daisy passed up and over the village.

The Weaver had brought light back to Cuddleton. Walker came to her side and smiled.

As the airship Daisy turned away from the growing helix of mighty tree trunks the boughs continued to spread far and wide overhead, the golden light bathing the entire Cuddle Vale.

Away from the crowds in a corner of the market square hidden in shadow a man dressed in black pushed back his hood revealing dirty red hair and a slightly rat-like face that was in dire need of a day in the sun and a good wash.

Billy Brand watched the airship speed away under the golden leaves with his mouth twisted into a scowl.

Holding up a piece of glass like a black mirror he waited until a face appeared in the reflection, it was distorted and wrapped in chains; his mysterious employer who sent only masked men to meet in shadows.

The crook said only one word, "Weaver."

PAPER CUTS

The walls of Castle Pandemonium were damp and black with mould as the corruption overtook the once vibrant fortress town and twisted it to a place of sorrow like a living malignance.

Queen Sola walked on threadbare carpets through the hallways, it did not matter that she was blind for she knew every path through her home. She did not notice the damp smell of the rot that was eating her furniture and tapestries, nor did she care that the tower and the city within the fortress walls were slowly crumbling to dust and ruin.

She muttered to herself in impotent rage at the lands beyond her walls; the foreigners, the spies, the people who wanted to take everything from her. They came to take it a piece at a time, bit by bit everything that was once beautiful and pure, they took those who were most precious to her and imprisoned her in this place.

Did they imprison her or had she closed herself away? Sola no longer knew any more, but she resented them all. Trespassers. Invaders. Vermin.

In the Grand Hall a long banquet table sat with a single chair at the end, food from a great feast still lay on platters uneaten and long since turned putrid.

To one side of the table was an enormous fire place that had not seen flame in a long time, ash from an extinct fire still lying cold in the hearth.

Crowded around the hearthstone were four creatures like blobs cloaked in black cloth from which a black mist seemed to drift. They had pale faces like porcelain masks or doll faces with empty black eye sockets.

Sola might have been blind but she knew they were hovering there and she knew exactly what they looked like, in her mind she could see them clear as day floating around the hearth watching her, the ones who told her the dark book would close the void if she summoned it.

They drifted across the Grand Hall to the Queen, gliding smoothly with their cloaks trailing on the ground leaving a path of dust as they went.

As they came to surround the Queen they spoke in whispers all at once.

"A Weaver is come."

"They will destroy us."

"They want to take this home."

"The Purse Loyal has found it."

"They will drive us from this place."

"Weaver."

"He says it is a girl."

"She will come for you."

"She will come for us all."

"These walls are not safe."

"She will take your children."

"Weaver."

"She must be stopped."

"She is coming."

"She is in the sky."

The whispers were unending, repetitive, maddening. They would not stop, the Queen turned but they were all around her.

"Weaver."

"She will take everything from you."

"She is coming."

The Weaver is in the sky, if that were the case then she could travel easily but was just as easily a target. The Queen would not let her come here. This was Sola's home, the Weaver was not welcome here, she had no place here.

"Stop her," the whispers said, "destroy her."

The Queen walked to the balcony that she knew looked out from the Tower over the courtyard and into the derelict city.

"Tell the Purse Loyal to track her," Sola said at last, "if he captures her he is to take her to the Pits of Flame and he will be rewarded."

"She must be knocked from the sky."

"She must be stopped."

"She is coming."

Whispers, whispers, always whispers. Haunting her. Always with her. Always in her ear. Endless whispers following her.

Throwing open the balcony door Queen Sola raised both hands into the air and she screamed in pain and anger as black paper birds wreathed in smoke shot from her arms and into a dark cloud forming overhead.

*

The airship Daisy drifted over the green fields and blue

streams that lined the valley as farmhands came out to tend to the crops under the new golden light.

Leaning over the rail of the ship Sophie watched as the entire valley came to life once more, whatever troubles the people may have had were put aside. What was the phrase Daddy used, make hay while the sun shines?

Looking at the sky above her she saw that the boughs of the golden trees had more or less stopped growing. Here and there a few a bright leaves continued to unfold but the pair of trees were now as big as they were going to get.

Sophie still had no idea how she had been able to make them sprout from nowhere and as she looked to the black smudge of night on the horizon she wondered if she would be able to do it all again.

"What is on your mind?"

Walker had come to stand next to her as she stared out across the dark mat of the Kingdom of Trancelvania still largely bathed in the night beyond, leaning his spindly arms on the railing and tilting his tricorne hat back.

"I'm wondering how exactly I'm supposed to save the Kingdom."

"We will save it," Walker nudged her, "you will not have to do it alone, it will be a team effort."

"Yes," she brushed her blonde hair back as it caught in the breeze, "but how, Walker? I think it is a bit beyond the power of a little girl to light a celestial furnace."

"I do not know," Walker finally admitted it, "truth be told I do not even know what caused the sun to vanish. The Oracowl pointed me in one direction and told me that I would meet a Weaver and together we would find one who was wise and one with a hidden strength."

"And then what?"

"It was kind of vague about that part," the clockwork man waved his hand in the air, "something about taking the darkness to free the light."

"Basically it pinched your rosy cheeks and said 'off you pop then'. That's just great."

"But you have already freed some light," he threw his hands into the air boldly, "the Cuddle Vale has not been so bright in days."

"Maybe, but it's still getting colder," Sophie said with a shiver and pulled her cloak tighter, "and trees lose their leaves in winter. I don't think this will last."

"Maybe that is why we need the Tome," Walker looked around, "where is Wikki anyway?"

They looked around the long deck of the airship but the walking book was nowhere to be seen. Walker was about to check below deck when Sophie gave a shout for Wikki to come down.

High up in the rigging that joined the boat to the blimp Wikki was stood on a large knot poking at the long balloon.

"It's amazing," he called out cheerily, "do you think Daisy can feel anything whilst she is like this?"

Sophie hadn't thought about that, somehow Daisy had stopped being a cow and became their airship. A groan came from the hull of the ship that sounded a little bit like a confused moo.

"Remember," Wikki shouted down as a warning, "this is an airship."

"I will," Sophie called back, "but you come down here, it's dangerous up there."

'Dear Lord' she thought to herself, 'I sound just like Mummy when I'm playing in a tree'.

The sky started to dull as if it were the evening time as the airship drifted from under the golden boughs of the trees and back into the night time lands. Sophie gave an unconscious shiver even though the air had not got any colder, feeling a chill at night was just something that she expected to happen.

"I'll be down in a minute," Wikki shouted as he swung from one knot to the next, "I only have a few more tests to carry out on our travelling companion."

She looked at Walker who gave a resigned shrug and turned back toward the horizon. It occurred to her that as a book Wikki would probably be fine if he were to fall from the rigging. The only way a fall could hurt a book would be if it were to break the spine, a morbid little fact that books shared in common with people she mused.

It did not take long for darkness to overtake the airship and Walker had to light lanterns along the deck. Beyond their craft the landscape was a dark blanket dotted with the occasional light of a farmstead but otherwise lit only by the colourful tapestry of stars.

Sophie had never seen stars shine so bright; it seemed to her almost as if they were trying to make up for the lack of sunlight. They lit up a milky cloud of colour that arched from one end of the horizon to the other.

"Where's the moon?"

Something had not seemed quite right about the sky since they had arrived here but until now Sophie had not been able to put her finger on just what. It was only now when she started to admire how beautiful the heavens were that it finally hit her.

"There it is," Walker pointed to a circle in the sky that was completely and unnaturally black, "it can be hard to spot sometimes. You just have to look for the void where there are no stars."

"Of course, without the sun there can be no moonlight," she said, remembering science class.

"The moon went black first, it happened over a year ago," Walker said, "obviously an omen for what was to come, but nobody has been able to explain it."

Sophie stared back at the black circle that hung like a sinkhole in the otherwise colourful sky, it reflected no light at all. She didn't know what that meant but it told her that whatever had happened to the sun wasn't natural. It was the work of somebody, or something.

That scared and encouraged her. If someone could black out the sun and the moon they were clearly powerful, however if it was the work of someone then that work could be undone. That gave her a glimmer of hope.

"Whoops!"

Turning their heads up they saw that Wikki had slipped and was hanging like one of those air fresheners shaped like a tree with his feet tangled in the rigging.

"I guess now I know what it would be like to live in a chained library," he said, swinging in the breeze, "I think I'm going to cough up some ink."

"Do you need help?"

Walker had started toward the main mast as Sophie went to the rope ladder strung from the blimp to the side rail.

"Nah," he said, swinging himself back and forth until he could grab the nearest rope ladder, "I think you guys will be too busy steering us around that ominous black cloud."

"What ominous black cloud?"

Turning as one Walker and Sophie saw a huge black mass on the dark horizon that was growing in size to blot out the starry sky.

"Oh, that ominous black cloud."

It wasn't just growing in size but it was definitely making its way toward them, lighting up inside with bright flashes and the rumble of thunder rolled out to reach them.

"Are you doing that?"

"I don't think so," Sophie could not be certain about anything related to these strange powers but she was pretty sure that she wasn't in the kind of mood that would whip up another storm, she'd been quite happy since they took to the sky, "this one feels different, not like before."

Walker turned back to the black cloud, it seemed to be spreading arms out on either side to surround them. Daisy's hull groaned with a sound like a frightened moo as Walker ran to the large wheel for steering the airship.

"It is moving too fast for us to turn," he shouted as he pushed the wheel forward and the bow of the ship dipped, "I am going to put us into a dive and hopefully we will pick up enough speed that we will be able to pull up and punch through it to come out above."

As the blimp passed below the cloud and the stars were hidden from them there was a crack of lightning overhead and a boom of thunder that was felt more than heard, a cosmic whip-crack that filled the air.

The wind began to rush on the deck as the airship got faster and faster, and Sophie had to hold on to the side rail. There was another noise in all the wind and thunder, it was a strange sound, a sort of fluttering like thousands of dried leaves blowing in the wind.

She looked up in fear for Wikki but saw that the Tome had tied himself on to one of the main rope ladders. He gave her a thumbs-up and an awkward smile to reassure her as he could see that she was a little bit unnerved, and was holding her Bunny for comfort.

The rapidly approaching ground ahead of Daisy was an uneven mess of shadows and looked to Sophie as if it might once long ago have been a town or city. But then the darkness hid many secrets.

A black swirl of something shot around the airship to the sound of rustling leaves. There was no doubt about it there was something hiding in that angry black cloud.

"Hold on tight," Walker shouted over a crushing boom of thunder, "here we go!"

Fighting to pull the wheel back Daisy's hull mooed in protest as her blimp angled upward and the ship strained against the rigging.

Sophie's knuckles were going white as she watched the horizon drop out of sight and the bow of the airship rose to point at the black maelstrom crackling with rage overhead.

"Come on, Daisy," she willed the airship to go faster, "you can do it."

From out of nowhere a tailwind caught Daisy and began pushing them faster upward and forward until suddenly they punched into the howling black cloud.

It had an awful choking smell like burning wood and everywhere around them were the rushing sounds of blown leaves speeding by. Each time the leaves shot past the airship there came the sound of thousands of tiny, angry screams. Like bats? Thousands of them.

"There's something in this cloud," Sophie shouted to Walker, "how soon until we get above it?"

"Should not be long," the clockwork man was straining every cog in his body to hold the wheel back, "just keep that wind behind us."

A stream of angry black leaves stormed between the blimp and the ship only narrowly missing Sophie as she dropped to the deck. She put her hands over her ears to block out the chorus of tiny, screaming voices.

There was a slap against the mast and something fell on the deck in front of her. It looked like a sheet of black paper that had been folded into the shape of a bird, it flapped about with a broken wing for a few moments before it turned to ash and blew away in the wind.

"What on earth?"

She slipped Floppsy Bunny back into her satchel and went to reach for the remains of the small pile of ash when she was forced to cover her ears again as another stream of paper birds screamed overhead.

And then the stars opened up around them.

Standing up Sophie looked across at Walker who now was leaning against the wheel and he gave her a strained thumbs-up. He was tired. He had felt a spring twang as he fought to keep the ship rising and would need to open himself up to reattach it before he tried to travel far. That would have to do until he could replace it.

But at least they were above that cloud now.

Sophie went back to the rail and looked down at the angry black mat below the airship, sparks of lightning still danced in it and she could hear the screams of the origami birds.

She knew that she wasn't the cause of that storm; someone or something else had done that.

Billy Brand, she thought, he must have done this. Was this the power of the Shadow People?

"That was intense," Wikki called down as he untied himself from the rigging of the blimp.

"What was that," Walker called as he propped his chest open and began working at his cogs, "have you ever heard of anything like that?"

"That was a very angry black cloud," Wikki untangled himself from the last of the ropes, "and I've never seen anything like it before."

"Those things inside it," Sophie was still watching the cloud storming beneath them, "they were like paper birds, they turned to ash if they got damaged."

A scream came up and an eruption of the origami birds burst from the storm and flowed like an angry river. It arched in the sky and slammed against the main rope over Sophie's head, thousands upon thousands of them clashing against the heavy rope and showering the deck in a blizzard of ash.

The screaming sound was relentless as they smashed upon the rope in countless number.

"Uh-oh," Wikki said.

Then before anyone could move the stream of paper birds cut through the rope and the ship tipped to one side.

Sophie cried out as she fell over the edge hearing Walker scream her name as she was swallowed up by the ferocious darkness.

"I'll find her," Wikki shouted down to the clockwork man, and then he threw himself from the blimp to plummet past the ship and plunge into the black unknown.

6

MUSHROOM! DEAD AHEAD!

"Ok, what do I do, what do I do?"

Daisy's steering wheel was more or less jammed in the forward position as the ropes linking it to the fins on her blimp were pulled tight after the main rope snapped.

The airship was listing badly to one side and was drifting down toward the menacing black cloud. Walker pulled back on the wheel and tried to turn it, and with another moo-like groan from the hull the ship gradually started to turn.

"That is it, Daisy," he said, "you can do it."

There was a bit of a clearing in that thunderous cloud; not an eye of the storm but more like a bubble from where it was starting to get wispy along the edge. If Daisy could just make it there he might be able to put her down safely.

Another screaming swarm of the black origami birds shot over his head, missing the airship entirely and diving back into the mists of the wicked cloud.

As he fought to hold course his mind drifted to Sophie, he hoped that she was alright. It was very brave of Wikki to jump after her, but Walker wasn't sure how much help the Tome would be, he had very quickly noticed that Wikki was all brains and very little common sense.

Another arc of those bird things dove at the airship but they broke apart harmlessly on the main deck sending up a cloud of ash.

"Ha," he shouted to no one in particular, "you missed!"

Another far bigger stream rose out of the cloud in front of the airship and had Walker had a throat he would have gulped. With a thousand tiny screams they charged toward him and at the last moment arched down and slammed into the same spot on the deck as before. Daisy's hull groaned in protest as a cloud of ash grew to cover the entire deck like a choking grey mist.

"Me and my big mouth," Walker tried to turn the ship away from the stream of paper birds whilst still trying to keep her more or less aimed for the clearing in the storm.

The force of the stream of angry origami was too much for the rigging to take and the forward ropes snapped and the bow of the vessel tipped forward.

As the deck tipped Walker grabbed the railing at the back of the ship, his feet slipping from under him and soon there was nothing but a long drop between him and that vicious black cloud.

The blimp above him was still carrying the airship on course toward the bubble of clear sky, against all odds they might still make it.

Climbing up and over the railing at the very back of the ship he looked down at the deck with the angry cloud passing beneath them and lightning crackling within.

Another flock of black origami birds screamed by, they almost missed entirely except for one that managed to give a paper cut to the blimp.

"Oh give me a break," Walker looked up at the small cut that was steadily hissing air like a balloon farting around a room.

Daisy started to drop very quickly, with the cow figurehead on the bow already scraping the top of the cloud, and then the black mist started to rise up the deck toward Walker.

"This is it, Daisy," he shouted, hoping that the cow wasn't able to feel anything as an airship, "prepare for crash landing!"

The airship gave one final groaned moo as they dropped into the smoky blackness of the storm.

*

Sophie awoke with a jump. She didn't hurt from her fall, she seemed to have landed in something that looked like an oversized bathroom sponge and which smelled like a sweaty gym sock, a solid hint to jump off if ever there was one.

It was hard to make out her surroundings, there were old stone walls around her that were open to a small window of stars overhead, and next to her there was something like a glass tree growing in the soft soil.

These must be the ruins that she had seen when the airship was diving to pick up speed, there had looked to be a vast sprawl of them beneath the shadow of the storm.

She looked back up and confirmed that the sky was indeed clear, and then had a quick moment of panic before she checked her satchel and was relieved to find that Floppsy Bunny was still there.

Unfortunately she had no way to know how long she had been asleep or unconscious, but she knew she was lucky to have landed on something so soft. When she looked around the sponge had vanished and all there was in its place was grass and a somewhat ripe smell. It may not have been luck, it could have been her Weaver powers or if she had known the term 'deus ex machina'.

Thankfully she was not sore but as she looked around to get her bearings she thought about Walker, Wikki and Daisy the cow. She had no idea where they might be now.

Walker would try to find her of course with the same 'all goal no plan' determination shared by chancers all across the universe. The question was would she be better staying here or starting off in the direction that they had been travelling?

Better to keep moving she decided, the others would have to travel back in order to find her so if she started forward they would be reunited sooner. It was the beginnings of a plan at least.

First of all she would have to get to higher ground so that she could figure out which direction would actually count as 'forward'.

Climbing over a pile of rubble that had once been a wall Sophie found that she was in what looked to be a wide street. The stones that made up the road were much larger than those in Cuddleton, and were light grey but covered in moss rather than years of trampled animal poo.

The buildings were all two storey with empty black windows and no roofs, rubble lay scattered about the street and the air was deathly silent.

It was unnerving walking up the avenue by herself, she felt like a little girl again but Sophie tried to take comfort in the fact that hearing no sounds meant that she was actually alone. She reached into her satchel to stroke Floppsy Bunny and she tried to imagine what it was that had happened here.

Had there been a war, or did everyone have to flee the city? Or did they just abandon it one day and it fell to ruin? Looking into some of the buildings she half-expected to see skeletons or something far worse, but the buildings were completely empty. There was no furniture, no pots or old kitchen utensils, no signs that this place had ever been lived in. Nothing but empty rooms with grass on the floor. She stepped back into the street and looked around again. She couldn't see any road signs or signs over shop doors, no abandoned carts, no broken jars. Had anyone ever even been to this place?

Why on earth would anyone build an empty city, did something happen that scared off the people before they could move here? Did some ambitious leader run out of money before they could finish their grand plan? Kings and Emperors did that sort of thing didn't they, build places to name after themselves like Constantinople, Washington, and... she tried to think of another- Dudley?

The ruins seemed to be getting taller in the direction she was taking, which she took to mean that she was getting near to the middle of the city. With a little bit of luck she might find a tower or something to check her bearings and then make her way toward Walker.

*

The stars were overhead, that was a good sign, right?

Before Walker could think a second thought something slobbered over his face, it felt like a wet leather sack being rubbed over him. Pushing it back and rubbing the slime off the glass lenses of his eyes the cogs within adjusted and the fuzzy blur in front of him became a brown cow.

"How now brown cow," he jumped up and threw his arms

around her neck, "I am glad you are alright, Daisy."

"Moo," she said weakly and Walker could see that she had damaged a hoof.

Apart from a small cut on her side she seemed to be no worse for the wear, although she was a little unsteady when she walked.

"You are not too bad, girl," he said as he took in their surroundings, a forest of giant mushrooms, "all things considered."

A line had been cut through the mushrooms behind them and ended in the small crater in which they now stood. Daisy must not have turned back into her true self until after the crash, which was probably why they were in pretty good shape. All things considered again.

A giant red with white polka dot cap of one mushroom had slid down the side of the crater and lay next to them. Daisy sniffed at the cap but kicked it away with a look of disgust.

"Not on the menu then," Walker started toward the gentle slope of the gouge from their crash, "let us see where we are and then we will look for Sophie."

The rift cut into the ground wasn't difficult for Daisy as she hobbled after Walker who for his part turned every few steps just to make sure that she was able to keep up.

He felt a little guilty that she was here; she had only been curious back in the village and now she was a country cow lost in the big wide world.

Daisy herself thought that the flight had been a bit of fun, up until the crash landing of course. Now she was wondering if she could ever go back to being a small town cow after soaring with the eagles?

Climbing to the spongy soil of the forest floor that seemed

to be mostly moss, the pair saw that the forest of red and white mushrooms stretched as far as the eye could see in every direction.

"Oh boy," there were no landmarks that Walker could see, everything was obscured but the heavens above and the mushrooms were doing their best to blot that out too, "I do not suppose that you know how to read the stars?"

"Moo," Daisy said, and then she started walking back in the direction pointed by the gouge in the forest floor.

"Well, we came that way," he followed suit, "Sophie must have fallen out here somewhere."

"Moo," Daisy confirmed.

The mushrooms swayed gently from whatever breeze happened to be going on above, their stems making a weird puff-slurp noise as they moved, like the sound of foam being squeezed.

It was quite peaceful under the huge caps wobbling beneath the stars, with the mossy ground their footsteps were silent and the big mushrooms had no leaves to rustle.

"I am sorry for getting you into this," Walker said to Daisy, mostly for his own benefit as Daisy was a cow and he doubted that she would understand.

"Moo," Daisy seemed to shrug as she walked, in matter of fact she understood seven languages and only two of them were cow.

"The Oracowl did not say anything about a cow," he continued, talking passed the time if nothing else, "it did not say much of anything actually. Seek out a Weaver, you will find her easily, then you must find someone wise and someone who is strong, and then our path would be laid before us. You know how sages speak."

"Moo?"

"I know," Walker looked down at his feet as they marched on, "I do not have any more idea now than I did then. And I have lost Sophie."

"Moo," Daisy said, reassuringly.

"That was magic that we were attacked by," he said, and then felt it would be a good time to check that his sword was undamaged, "somebody sent that storm after us, after the Weaver."

He stopped in his tracks and Daisy turned to look back at him, their eyes met and he broke into a run. Somebody was after the Weaver, and they had found her.

"We have to hurry."

7

MAGIC PUDDLE ON THE FLOOR

"Oh, wow," Sophie said as she stared up into the starry sky.

An enormous stone tower stood before her, taller than anything that she had ever seen before, it was like a giant needle of granite trying to burst the balloon that was the sky.

The grounds around it seemed to be a vast, open plaza that Sophie realised must once have been a pond but had long ago dried up. At the far shore was a funny white building like something out of a movie, it was all columns and domes and probably exploded in fairly spectacular fashion.

Looking back at the tower Sophie reckoned that if she wanted to get a good view of the countryside then this was the place to be. She walked around the huge stone needle until finally finding a surprisingly small and unassuming door.

Well it would have been a door but the wood had vanished leaving only two heavy hinges and a metal hoop of a handle rusting on the ground outside.

Stepping across the threshold she saw that the tower was hollow and lit by a greenish blue light from somewhere far above. Around the walls inside wound a spiral staircase that climbed all the way into the dizzying heights of the tower.

"That, is a lot of stairs," Sophie slumped her shoulders, she had forgotten that going up would mean a lot of climbing.

"Umm, let down your hair?"

Well, it was worth a shot.

When her eyes dropped from the greenie blue glow far above to the grey stone walls she saw that an elevator had appeared out of nowhere.

It was one of those old fashioned brass contraptions with doors like a metal fence, lit with a warm orange light and its walls finished in a plush red velvet that screamed 'posh'.

Out of nowhere a tall thin man in a fancy red uniform trimmed in gold and looking like a waiter who had been decorated many times for decanting under fire slid open the brass gates.

"Good evening, Miss," he removed a red hat trimmed with golden laurels and gave a small bow of his head, "going up?"

"Uh, yes," Sophie paused before accepting the Porter's invitation, "thank you."

"My pleasure, Miss," he closed the gates behind them and when he pushed a brass leaver forward the elevator began to rise, "are you enjoying your visit to our fine city?"

"I've only just… landed," she eyed him, he seemed to be a personable sort of chap, "actually I'm not even sure where here is."

"Oh my," he chuckled, "a fine day to get lost. Don't worry, your feet will soon find their way."

The elevator looked out into the tower as it rose toward the strange light above, the spiralling staircase zipping across Sophie's vision before curling back out to the other side of the tower then curling back in again.

"What is this tower anyway?"

"The Tower of Tahl, home of the Grand Magus," the Porter replied, "it's one of the oldest buildings in all of Trancelvania."

"Grand Magus? Is that like a wizard?"

"Oh yes, Miss, the highest level of wizard in the land."

"Is that why his tower is so big," Sophie asked, remembering Walker having mentioned Wizard Towers back in Cuddleton, "do bigger towers mean higher rank?"

"Officially size doesn't matter," the Porter turned and gave her a knowing smile, "magic has an odd effect on people, it tends to stunt growth. Generally the more powerful the magic the shorter the wizard, so they tend to... overcompensate a bit."

"Oh," she remembered how the shortest boys in school were universally the loudest.

She was silent for a few moments as the walls in the tower grew brighter and brighter as they neared the high source of the light. A thought was nagging at her though, the Porter was the first person she had seen since she had got here, living or otherwise.

"Are you this Grand Magus?"

"No, Miss," the Porter looked at her quizzically, "why on the stars would you think that?"

"This entire city is in ruin," she said, "apart from grass that has obviously grown back everything that might once have been living has disappeared."

"I don't understand," the Porter was looking at Sophie as if she had transformed into a lobster and started speaking in a bad Afro-Caribbean accent.

"You are the only alive person here," she said as the elevator passed behind a solid wall, "do you not think that's maybe a bit strange?"

"Miss, I have no idea what you are talking about," he looked genuinely confused as the elevator stopped at a huge bright room and he opened the brass gates.

"There is nobody else in this entire city," Sophie said as she stepped out into the chamber, "nobody."

She turned and saw that the elevator was gone, not lowered just gone. Even the shaft had disappeared and had been replaced by the same grey stone walls that made up the rest of the tower.

"I need to figure out how I'm doing that," she said to nobody, and trying to disregard the fact that she had essentially just had a full blown conversation with a figment of her imagination, she was fairly certain that people got locked up in padded rooms for that sort of thing, "now, where's that window?"

The big, round room had a lot of strange metal equipment and laboratory apparatus lying on piles arranged in tidy lines around the floor. Sophie assumed that shelves had previously stood here but had vanished along with everything else that had not been made of metal or stone.

The weird greenie blue light seemed to be coming directly from the stones themselves that formed the ceiling. It wasn't a pleasant colour and something about it made Sophie feel uncomfortable; it reminded her of sickness, like that green stuff that she had been coughing up. But glowing.

This level must have been a store or library room and didn't have any windows. There was however another spiral staircase curling in the opposite direction to the main staircase in the tower, and there was more of that sickly light glowing from the hole in the ceiling that the stairs went through.

Removing Floppsy Bunny from her satchel for a comforting distraction she stepped slowly up the stairwell being sure to keep an eye on the darker opening the stairs passed through. The light in the room beyond looked to be more green than blue and the walls had a strange metallic sheen as if they were under those lights that made dust, teeth and stains glow.

Passing through the hole in the ceiling was like taking a momentary bath in light, there was a tingling feeling from it like getting goosebumps and it made a slight crackling or buzzing sound as she stepped through. It was like walking through static.

The room above was just as large as the one below and had many tall windows open to the night sky, but what was most striking was the huge pond of light in the middle of the room. The greenie blue light swirled and rippled like it was water and sometimes little whirls of the fluid-light would arch out or pop like bubbles.

The enormous room was entirely empty apart from the weird pond of light and its ceiling stretched up into a dark point far above.

This was definitely the top of the tower, but what was the purpose of this place? The glow wasn't bright enough for it to be a lighthouse, and she was pretty sure that they were built near the sea and not in the middle of a city.

She stepped to the edge of the strange pool and knelt down beside it. Her skin glowed in a strange grey colour from the light and white specks of dust shone like bright freckles, it did not feel any warmer to be this close but the tingling feeling was much stronger.

Leaning down toward the light and stretching her fingers forward Sophie want to see if there was any feeling or substance to the pool.

"Oh I wouldn't do that, child," a voice said that nearly caused her to jump back like a startled cat, "the mana well will blast the spirit right out of your body."

Sophie looked around trying to see the man who had spoken. Eventually she saw him walking in the shadows, a short little man with stumpy legs who appeared to be mostly belly and pointy hat.

He was also dead. She assumed so anyway since he seemed to be a ghost.

Aside from the warning to Sophie he completely ignored her. Instead he was babbling away to himself and was walking from one pile of broken glass and metal to another and moving his hands as if working with equipment that was no longer there. She wondered if he could see the ghost of the tables and apparatus, or if he was just stuck in some kind of a mental loop and was so absorbed in what he was doing that he was too busy to realise that he was dead.

"Are you the Grand Magus?"

The ghost didn't respond to her, instead waving his hands in the air as if conjuring a spell, or chasing away a particularly irritating gnat. All that happened though was that a few sparks flashed in the air and there came a mournful squeaking noise like a balloon slowly having the air let out. Could a ghost cast spells, or was this the ghost of magic past?

"Hmm, that didn't work," he said as he walked obliviously through Sophie, she caught a glimpse of a little balding head with a few scattered remnants of a bad comb-over as she looked down through the hat.

"How rude," she would have knocked that silly hat off his head had it not been about as substantial as a politician's integrity.

"Maybe if I try to summon..." he waggled his fingers to which a bubble formed in the mana well and burst with a loud pop.

"Rats," he kicked an imaginary stone with a stubby little foot at the end of an equally stubby leg.

Looking down at the swirling mana well Sophie started to suspect that it had something to do with why all the people, wood, paper and animals had disappeared. Obviously it was some form of concentrated magic, but there was something that was just inherently wrong with it.

The surface of the pool became like glass in front of her and changed to show a beautiful city, all high towers and bustling with life. Thousands of people, so many small shops and traders, markets on the streets into the city, churches and schools, children playing on a bright and sunny day.

The image on the pool changed to show the needle-like tower of the Grand Magus, glorious and white, shining like a jewel. Inside she saw the Magus in his silly big hat talking to someone who looked like a Mayor, what with the rotund body and suit of a board game mascot over which was draped a gold chain like an angry rapper, and a regal lady who very much had the presence of a Queen. The crown on her head was a big hint.

The Magus was showing them something on a chart, it looked like some kind of vortex or whirlpool hovering over a valley with the darkened moon overhead. The group looked from one to another concerned and after talking at length came to some form of agreement, then the Mayor and Queen left taking copies of the chart each.

Left by himself staring down into the mana well on the floor the Grand Magus was now looking directly at Sophie. It was almost as if he knew that she was there, could somehow see the girl in a woman's body staring back at him across the span of time, space or reality.

His eyes were heavy and he gave her a slow nod before walking away. He knew that his plan would fail or why else would he be looking at a Weaver.

The image on the mana well got brighter, then dimmer then brighter again several times, and on each brighter moment the Magus looked on at Sophie. He was getting unkempt, his neat little moustache getting untidy and his eyes were hollow. It was showing the passage of days, each day checking back to see if she was still there, that he would still fail.

Suddenly the image changed to outside the tower in the late evening. Four black blobs came out of nowhere across the sky and began to circle the tower and leaving a swirling black cloud forming in their trail.

Inside the tower the world outside looked black. The Grand Magus stood at one side of the mana well as the four shadowy creatures flew in to land at the other, their faces like porcelain masks with empty eyes.

The Magus raised his hands in the air and magic burst from his fingertips but the wispy things were too nimble, again and again he fired balls of lightning as they dodged around, it was as if they were playing with him.

Tentacles of black mist drifted from their bodies as they surrounded him, it drifted up into his nose, ears, and mouth. The Magus started to choke.

Falling to his knees as his eyes turned black he raised his hands again into the air. Sophie watched in horror as the mana well in the image rose in a ball of blue light out of the pool to hover before him.

She saw a single tear in his eye and then the ball exploded.

The image showed his body simply vanish and his blue ghost be thrown against the wall. Then it showed the enormous blast of green energy shooting out from the tower disappearing people, animals, food, plants, carts, doors, anything made of wood.

And then any buildings with wooden supports started to collapse in clouds of dust.

Sophie had her hand over her mouth as she looked up from the terrible scenes unfolding in the well to the ghost of the Magus in the corner of this tower that had become his tomb, still fiddling with phantom spells.

"They made you kill the city," she could barely say the words, she felt so sorry for the poor man. No wonder his spirit was as out of his mind as well as his body.

"I think you've seen enough," a voice said as she was suddenly yanked backward, "hello, Stinky Sophie."

She turned in shock as Billy Brand wrapped a rope around her wrists before she could react. He looked older but she still recognised the thin nose, freckled face and dirty ginger hair. He was dressed in a black hooded tunic with a dark grey hooded cloak, and had a long, thin sword hanging by his side in a scabbard that was also hooded.

"Get off me, Billy Brand," she struggled too late, "you pig of a boy."

"See this sword by my side, Stinky," he yanked the rope, hurting her wrists, "don't make me use it."

He started toward the stairwell that led down to the empty storeroom, giving the rope the same kind of tug that one would give a leash when your dog has found a particularly enchanting stain on a lamppost.

Sophie found it odd that despite him wearing black there were not any bright white specks of dust showing up under the black light glow of the mana well, it was almost as if he was absorbing the light.

"Where are you taking me?"

"We're going on a little journey," he looked back over his shoulder with a wicked grin, "to the Pits of Flame in the shadow of Mount Bad."

"I'm guessing that isn't a holiday resort," she tried to wrench her wrists free from his bonds but the knots were too tight. Seems that there was something that he was actually good at other than getting first years to eat ladybugs.

"No," he yanked again as he pulled her toward the main stairwell that led down the tower, "it is not."

He already had a long length of rope tied to an outcropping of rock that for some reason just happened to exist in the tower, he kicked the main bundle over the edge and it took a few seconds that felt more like minutes before the rope snapped taut.

"I am not climbing down that," she said in a way that implied her hands were on her hips.

Billy Brand smiled wickedly and said, "You're right."

And then he knocked Floppsy Bunny from her hands and

pushed her screaming over the edge into the long black fall.

&.

THE CHASE IS ON

Jumping off the airship had seemed like a good idea at the time, back when there was a dark cloud and reckless bravado hiding the world beneath. When he was through the storm and with the ground now suddenly rushing toward him Wikki was beginning to feel like a bit of a tit.

He held his pages wide open like a parachute and was able to more or less aim himself toward what looked to be a fairly soft patch of ground. Relatively speaking.

On the second bounce he knew that the ground wasn't that soft.

"Ah, Ras Alhague," he said with a pained sigh as he lay on his back staring up at the stars as the black storm cloud mysteriously cleared, "head of Ophiuchus. Forty six point seven light years away, surface temperature eight thousand five hundred Kelvin." (p81 of Sir P. M. Xylophone's *The Existential Dread of an Endless, Empty Universe*)

Letting out a long breath he then checked the scuffs on his cover and dog ears on his pages.

"That hurt."

Standing up he brushed off a few small stones that were stuck in the old leather of his cover and wished that he had the foresight to have brought a dust jacket.

"Strangely quiet," he looked about at the grey stone ruins in the area around him, "there should be cicadas chittering at this longitude."

Pulling a sextant from within his pages he took a couple of readings of the stars and orientated himself against the glow on the horizon coming from Cuddleton.

"Ok, by my calculations this should be the City of Slumberg," he tried to compare with what he was seeing with what knowledge he had of the city, "it should be in a somewhat better state of repair than this."

The ruins remained silent in response.

Wikki assumed that the first thing Sophie would do would be to try and find a high point, to see if she could figure out what direction they had been travelling and maybe see where Daisy had landed.

Like most town there would be a mage's tower somewhere near the centre because they like to be nothing less than the centre of attention, and on his way down he was fairly certain that he saw something that fit that very description.

The sickly green light that he'd seen coming from said tower probably didn't mean anything at all. Some towers just glowed with death magic. Perfectly normal.

He started off at a brisk pace all the same.

*

Sophie screamed all the way down in what seemed like an endless freefall, the light of the mana well having long faded to a far distant pinpoint.

There was nothing but blackness below her and it seemed to stretch off into an eternity. She had definitely been falling for far longer that she had been in the elevator going up.

And then she hit the ground. Hard.

"Ouch," she said, still faceplanted on the cold, grey stone.

Surely a mattress or something was supposed to have appeared by some miraculous coincidence just before she hit the ground, was that not how this Weaver thing was supposed to work?

Slowly she pushed herself up, she was sore and she felt that she had grazes on her knees but apart from that there was no pain that she couldn't just walk off. Which in the circumstances was almost as good as a mattress.

Dusting her tunic down with her hands still tied she looked at the rope hanging next to her, it was whipping about as something moved along it.

As she was trying to work herself loose from the bonds around her hands Billy Brand appeared beside her on the rope hanging like a spy breaking into a vault.

"Well, look at that," he dropped to his feet, a smug grin on his face, "you made it."

Sophie tried to swing a punch at Billy Brand but he grabbed the loose end of the rope around her hands and yanked her off balance.

"Now, play nice," he said, starting toward the small door in the side of the tower, "we have a long walk ahead of us, if I have to tie your feet and make you hop the whole way I will."

She stared daggers at him in response but grudgingly followed, she would have to bide her time until she had a chance to get away.

The air outside had gotten noticeably cooler, not to the point that she could see her breath but there was now a definite chill on the breeze. Without the sun winter was coming.

"This way," he tugged on her rope and started off in the opposite direction from where she had originally fallen from the airship, toward the dark mountains conveniently looming in the distance for dramatic effect.

That was more or less the direction they had been heading, Sophie thought as she trudged up the deserted streets behind her captor. With any luck Billy Brand might lead her straight to Walker and the others and then Walker would punch him in his stupid face.

She wondered about the whole 'Shadow People' thing, certainly Billy Brand didn't seem to be any more special than the underachieving bully she knew him to be, and he certainly didn't appear to be a vampire as the lady in the inn had said. Sophie always did think of him as a bloodsucker, but more like a tick or a gnat. She definitely had not seen any sign of him being able to do any of the things that she was somehow doing.

If anything he seemed to be more like a rogue, which would be about right, only now he was bigger and armed to the teeth. She found as she too was bigger that she was less afraid of him, he didn't seem so frightening when they were about the same size, and when she thought about it that made her feel a bit bigger still.

But that left the more pressing question, if he was not able to do the things that she could then who created that storm that had battered Daisy and seemed to have purposefully lashed out to throw her overboard?

If it wasn't Billy Brand then somewhere out there was someone far worse and far more powerful, and they were after her.

She shivered.

*

Wikki had to make a pit-stop for a breath halfway up the winding staircase inside the Tower of the Grand Magus. His pages were ruffled from the fall and he grudgingly had to accept that he wasn't a recent edition anymore.

As he sat with his legs dangling out over the void he found himself wondering what had happened to Slumberg. This was one of the largest cities in the Kingdom and was a major trading point (p2931 of Horace J Postlethwaite's *The Condensed Geopolitical and Socio-Economic History of The Kingdom of Trancelvania and Lands Near and Far with which it Trades, vol. 4, abridged*). It was built on the crossroads leading from the country towns to the Capitol and the Sugar Road, so named for the main trade product along the route that wound away to near mystical far off lands. As well as closer and more mundane places where they wore sensible clothing and weren't all that interesting to talk about.

He also wondered idly why there was a rope hanging next to him. He knew about feng shui and aesthetics and all sorts of New Age nonsense but one random rope in a spire made about as much sense as one of those rooms filled with lots of clinking chains and constant dripping water.

He gave it a flick and it just flopped about loosely. Ok, so it wasn't anchored to anything down below. So what was it, easy access for a circus performer?

Wikki had met the Grand Magus once and athletic the wizard was not. The Magus stood nearly six feet tall and about the top four feet of which was hat. He had a round little body under his blue robes and a bad comb-over that itself was making a tactical retreat in the face of male pattern baldness.

Basically the Grand Magus had the physical prowess of a jam sandwich and was not the kind of guy to view ropes as a reasonable form of travel unless they were hooked up to some form of pulley arrangement.

Which more likely than not meant that somebody else had travelled it.

Wikki looked up at the greenish blue light above and knew immediately it was the candescence of the mana well glowing through the stone, but that somehow it had been tainted.

He feared for Sophie's safety more so than before, there was something very wrong about all of this. He couldn't fathom what kind of monstrous force it would take to corrupt a font of pure magical energy but evil was abroad, and much closer to home too.

He broke into a run up the winding stairs taking them in jumping strides that were bigger than his little legs would normally have carried him. He ran as fast as he could, so fast that the pages of his insides flapped with the wind.

He reached the rope anchored to the stone at the top and saw a room with lots of smashed equipment but no shelves.

And lying next to the rope was the toy bunny that the Weaver carried everywhere.

"Oh no."

Picking up the bunny he carefully stashed it into the pocket on the inside of his back cover and then started up the nearby stairwell that led to the top of the tower.

That sickly light was everywhere in this room, shining from a pool in the middle of the chamber like a glowstick had walked by and vomited in a pond.

"A font of concentrated mana," Wikki said as his pages glowed under the light of the mana well, "but you should be blue not green, this is a serious corruption."

"Tainted by death," the ghost of the Magus said in an offhanded way as he idly walked by on some phantom errand, "the nightmares imbued it with their evil."

"Grand Magus," Wikki jumped in shock as the phantom drifted by, he could do nothing but stare at the shade of what was once the most powerful wizard in Trancelvania.

The apparition paid the Tome no further heed than he had paid Sophie, continuing on some unseen spell or incantation, caught in the loop of reliving his final memories as if his spirit didn't want to accept the truth.

"Grand Magus, what happened to you?"

The wizard did not acknowledge him but continued mumbling words that sounded like a failed attempt to clear his throat and Wikki took a step back for fear of having his pages coated in a sneeze of ectoplasm.

"What nightmares?"

This time the Magus paused in his distracted reverie, a thought finally managed to bubble through the mess that remained of his once razor sharp mind.

"A sickness," he said, walking to where the chart had stood in Sophie's vision, "a sickness that has found its way through from the void."

"Void," Wikki tried to follow the Magus but he had resumed his random gibberish, "what is the void?"

"A growing absence," the Magus gave a dainty little wave of his fingers, "created by a force from the outside and it let the nightmares in."

That wasn't actually any more use than the other

explanations that he had offered. Nightmares were manifestations of negative emotions that were a dreamer's mind attempting to categorize and compartmentalize feelings in some manageable understanding. Wikki checked his pages but couldn't see how dreams would be able to manifest as a sickness.

Looking at the swirling mana well he had a hope that it might reveal some secret to him. It let a bubble pop on its surface to say that it had nothing to add on the subject.

"I saw a Weaver," the ghost looked down into the pool, "as soon as I saw her I knew that I was doomed to fail. No matter what I would do the nightmares would come, and they did."

"Whatever these nightmares are she might be the only one who can stop them," Wikki looked sadly to the defeated phantom of the Magus.

"Perhaps, or she has woven them herself," the wizard looked down at his transparent hands, "I'm dead, aren't I?"

"I'm afraid so," Wikki wondered if Sophie could undo the evil that had taken place here, "what do you mean that she could have woven them herself?"

"The Weavers are so called because they have an intrinsic power to weave our world. Something caused the void in the weave and loose strands are tangling into random horrors," the Grand Magus was perfectly lucid now, but since he realised that he was dead his spirit was starting to fade away to the afterweave.

"I think I'm going to go now," he faded until all that remained was the outline of his hat, "help her to see the light when the darkness comes."

"Wait," Wikki ran forward, "what is that supposed to

mean?"

There was no answer and he was left with only the sickly green glow from the corrupted mana well.

"Now what?"

"Just one more thing," the ghost popped back into existence like a sudden afterthought, "the Weaver was grabbed by someone dressed all in black, only the Shadow People and writers have such mundane fashion sense."

"Uh, thanks."

The Grand Magus had already vanished again leaving Wikki to worry about what villainy a Shadow Person could be up to, nothing good to be sure. And the thought occurred that he'd need to get a move on.

"Oh," he suddenly jumped to his feet as he remembered why he had come up here in the first place, "the window."

He jogged around the mana well and peered out the large window looking toward the black monoliths of the distant mountains. Daisy had been travelling in roughly that direction before the storm of paper birds, if she'd went down then that's where the others would be. If Sophie had been taken by one of the Shadow People then he had to get back to them quickly.

Everything in the distance was shrouded in night and there weren't any visible landmarks to get his bearings, one dark splodge looking much the same as any other. Closer to the tower however he could make out a few features of the landscape under the glittering starlight.

The buildings behind the tower seemed to get smaller rather quickly and were spaced further apart. He could see the broken walls of the Chancellery and a few defensive towers no longer fit for purpose as they lay fallen into the empty farmsteads that they were supposed to be defending.

Beyond the farms was a weird landscape that looked like a huge ball pit, balls as far as the eye could see.

As Wikki's eyes adjusted to the low light he was able to make out thick stalks coming from the balls, no, not balls... caps.

"Mushrooms, a forest of amanita muscaria maximus," he exclaimed (p12 of I. Tripp's unfinished *All Mushrooms are Psychedelic with the Right Attitude*), "Super Fly Agaric!"

He was scanning his eyes across the amazing field of massive red and white mushrooms when he spotted a weird empty patch pointing like a compass needle in his direction.

It was like something heavy and moving fast, possibly boat shaped had crashed into it like a meteor strike.

"Daisy, Walker," he said with glee as he ran back around the sickly mana well and back down the stairs to the store level. He grabbed the rope hanging out over the void to the base of the tower and took one quick and not at all vertigo inducing look down.

"I'm coming guys," he called out to no one in particular but it seemed like the thing to do and then taking a loose grip he jumped over the edge forgetting that he wasn't a Navy Seal.

*

"Come on," Billy Brand yanked at the rope tied around Sophie's hands.

She was walking deliberately slow to annoy him, also to give Walker and the others a better chance of finding her, but mostly it was to annoy.

When they had reached the edge of the city they had came across a weird forest of giant red and white mushrooms at which Billy Brand took one look and decided nope, Sophie quietly reflected to herself that he was not a fun guy and allowed herself a quiet giggle.

So now they were skirting around the edge of the forest and she was quite certain no longer heading toward Walker and the others.

The only thing that she could think to do was drag her heels and quietly kick over any stones or twigs that might form some kind of a trail. She'd lost Floppsy Bunny when she'd been pushed from the top floor of the tower, she could only hope one of the others made it that far and found him. She couldn't leave him in this strange land. Maybe he'd guide the others to her, she thought with the infallible logic of one who didn't comprehend that no one else could speak the secret tongue that existed between a child and a favourite toy.

Billy Brand didn't say much as they marched along, and when he did speak it was either an order or an insult. He really was a bit of a turd to be around.

Sophie didn't know how long that they had been walking when they came upon a dark valley with a dusty dirt path that led into a maze of dry canyons.

"I am not going in there," she said, stopping indignantly by an old dried up tree.

"Excuse me," he looked back with his rat face in a sneer showing his crooked teeth, "you don't have a choice in the matter."

"You'll just have to drag me because I am not going," she sat cross-legged on a stump and stared angrily at her captor.

Billy Brand briefly slouched his shoulders before a shadow crossed his face and he drew his long, thin sword.

"Now listen to me you annoying little wench," he stomped toward her with evil in his eye, "you are going to get up off your- aargh!"

Flailing his arms at his face he swiped and swiped in a panic all because he'd walked into an old cobweb that hung from the tree. It was quite funny to watch.

"Get it off get it off get it off!"

Billy Brand is afraid of spiders? As that thought occurred to Sophie the surly spider she first met outside of Cuddleton popped into her head. And a few seconds later popped into existence in front of her, only he was about three feet bigger than the last time that they'd met.

"What the web?"

The confused spider looked around, an act that didn't take long with eight eyes, some of which fell on Sophie with a look of slightly befuddled recognition. The rest of his eyes were watching the weirdo dressed in black who was jumping around making all the fuss.

"Here, pipe down there, boy," he said.

"Spider!" Billy Brand's eyes fell upon the waist high spider that stood between him and his erstwhile captive and they promptly went wide, "Big. Fat. Hairy. Spider!"

"Who are you calling fat, you cheeky little sod."

The spider started flicking hair from his abdomen with the speed and accuracy of throwing knives at the panic stricken boy who was going whiter and fuzzier by the second. The spider marched forward on his first three pairs of legs and throwing urticating hair with the back pair until fear finally got the better of Billy Brand and he ran away screaming.

The spider stopped when the boy ran around a large outcropping of stone and he turned to the girl with an eight eyed frown, his back legs ready to throw more needlelike hairs.

"Do you want some?"

"No," she held up her hands in peace and the spider's expression softened when he saw that she was tied up, "sorry for bringing you here, I needed some help."

"I see you are already webbed," the old spider clip-clipped over to her and began working at the ropes with his pedipalps, "let's see about... there we go."

The bonds fell away from Sophie as he stepped back with as much of a smile as possible on a thorax and she rubbed at where her wrists had gone a little red, but otherwise she was delighted.

"Thank you, Mr Spider."

"Call me Archie," he gave a slight bow, "you said that you brought me here, so I assume the rumours are true and there really was a Weaver in Cuddleton."

"I guess so," she said, "I really don't know what it means or how I can do the things that I have been doing, but I'm starting to understand what the term 'unintended consequences' means."

"Well, what were you doing when you brought me here?"

"Panicking about the nasty guy with the sword."

"What else," Archie sat down, crossing four legs and leaning his chin on the other four, pedipalp stroking a fang thoughtfully, "the strands of any web must all connect to make the whole. What were the strands of the moment that made me appear?"

"Well, Billy Brand was coming toward me in a not very friendly way when he walked into a cobweb and panicked," she looked up, "and I thought it was funny that the boy who bullied me at school was afraid of spiders, and then I thought about you chasing me away and I wished that you were here to teach him a lesson. And then you appeared. Only, you know, bigger."

Archie the spider smiled as Sophie's eyes lit up, she'd wished for it to happen and it did, like a genie without the lamp and not having to be the colour of a choking incident.

She turned her eyes to the sky with a look of determination, she stood up tall and raised her hands.

"I wish for the sun to shine again," and then she closed her eyes before she would be blinded.

After a couple of seconds she opened them and saw a bit of an anticlimax.

"I *really* wish for the sun to shine again," she strained her hands, spreading her fingers and gritting her teeth, "really, *really*."

"I don't think it's that simple."

"Oh poo," Sophie let out a breath that she didn't realise she had been holding. She put her hands on her hips and took her frustration out on a nearby stone with a sharp kick.

"I'm sure you'll work it out," Archie came and put two leg tips on her shoulder, "I imagine that it's no easy task restarting nuclear fusion in a star, there are quirks of gravity and hydrogen to consider. That's a lot of strands to connect in that web, maybe practice on something smaller first?"

"The web," she repeated, "web. Oh lordy, how am I going to get you home?"

All of a sudden they were standing in the shade of a brightly lit forest filled with fluffy webs, the same forest outside of Cuddleton where her adventure had first began.

Archie was back to his normal size once more and was sitting on the nearest branch.

"You'll get it, Miss Weaver," he said with a smile between his fangs and gestured around him, "you can do it without thinking. It will just take you some time."

"Thank you for your help, Archie," she said, now slightly distracted by having somehow blinked her way back across the Kingdom.

"Safe travels, Miss Weaver," he gave a small curtsy before opening the door to his web, "feel free to call again if you need any help, you have the friendship of arachnids."

Sophie smiled and started to walk through the forest, following the golden light of the trees overhead and hoping that she was going more or less in the direction of Cuddleton, and wondering how the heck she was going to find Walker now.

.9

HERE BE MONSTERS

Time as they knew it had lost all meaning for Walker and Daisy as the pair trudged through the mossy terrain, surrounded on all sides by the seemingly endless forest of giant mushrooms swaying hypnotically in the breeze overhead. In the Long Night it was like being in a sensory deprivation tank, or a lecture on accounting methodology at the revenue service.

Daisy seemed fairly certain about where she was going, occasionally stopping to sniff the ground before looking back at her companion and giving a reassuring snort.

It still was strangely quiet in the shade of the giant caps, as if something had scared all life from this place. Walker regarded the thick stalks of the mushrooms around him and added an appendix to his thoughts; all life that had the presence of mind to make like a tree and leave.

Idly he played his fingers over the hilt of his cutlass. No sign of immediate threat in the area was worse than being a lady of contract romance in Victorian London when guys who suffixed their name with 'the ripper' were around. But at least when people moved into a place and began to set up shop you would have a fair idea of what to expect; people got everywhere like sand in your undies and the subsequent infection. When people were giving an area a wide berth you had to ask why, and the answer usually wasn't anything good.

Men would march valiantly across fields of skulls and broken glass on the promise of golden idols or scantily clad Amazonians, a lack of humans meant that something bigger, badder, and worse smelling had recently passed through.

Daisy suddenly stopped stock still with her eyes narrowed and looking straight ahead, her ears perked up like radar towers.

"What is it, girl," Walker knelt next to her, wishing that the ground wasn't so soft or lacking in convenient twigs for an approaching antagonist to snap, "someone coming?"

She nodded silently as Walker strained to hear whatever whisper of a sound that Daisy had picked up on.

Somewhere directly in front of them he could just about make out a fast, muffled patter of someone running on the spongy earth and the feet were getting closer very quickly, presumably with the rest of their owner.

He was in the process of drawing his cutlass when something heavy slammed into him and he was knocked onto his back with a cry of "Zoikes!"

A book! Some cheeky bastard threw a book at him.

Daisy looked down as he struggled with the weight across his chest. She licked her lips helpfully.

"Walker?"

"Wikki?"

"Daisy," Wikki jumped off his fallen companion and

hugged the happy brown cow, "I'm glad to see that you guys survived the crash."

"Crashes seem to follow you," Walker said as he picked himself off the ground and dusted tufts of moss from his cape, "I take it that you could not find Sophie?"

Wikki turned to his companion with a crestfallen look, Walker knew a look of bad news before the Tome could even open his back pocket and pull out Floppsy Bunny.

Walker took the stuffed rabbit without a word and somewhere in his cogs a gear missed.

"I found it in the Tower of the Grand Magus in Slumberg," Wikki said as Daisy nuzzled her head against him in pity, "the ghost of the Magus told me that she was taken by one of the Shadow People."

"The Shadow People," Walker's eyes visibly darkened as if someone had turned a dimmer switch in his head. He knew all the stories about the Shadow People, "Now what do they want with a Weaver?"

"The Magus was talking about nightmares from a void, and that some kind of sickness had come from it," the Tome said, "to be honest he wasn't really talking an awful lot of sense, but he did seem to think that there was a possibility that Sophie could be weaving them herself."

"No," Walker dismissed it immediately, "I brought Sophie here myself because the Kingdom was already in darkness, it can't be her doing it."

"Maybe the Shadow Person is taking her to these nightmares?"

"Moo."

Walker looked at Wikki and then to Daisy, and then back to Wikki once more for good measure.

The nightmares whatever they were, that was something

that they would have to worry about later, if they were even real, the gang only had the word of a ghost and his haunted puddle for that.

The Shadow People on the other hand were as real as a fungal infection and if one of them had taken Sophie then the Weaver was in serious trouble.

But if Wikki had followed them from Slumberg then Sophie and her captor hadn't made it this far, maybe the Purse Loyal hadn't wanted to take her through the vast sprawl of mushrooms.

"Come on," Walker slipped Floppsy Bunny into his own satchel, "we haven't heard anyone coming this way, let's see if we can pick up their trail back at the forest edge."

*

Sophie wasn't sure if she had passed this way before.

The massive branches of her golden trees were overhead and it definitely felt like she was heading toward Cuddleton, but in daylight, or treelight this place did not look familiar.

Her plan was to get back to the village and try to pass unnoticed so that she could work out which direction the airship had been going, and then do an awful lot of walking. That was Plan A.

Plan B was B for Blink, as in blink and be back with Walker. The problem with that plan was that she still wasn't quite able to grasp how she was doing, well... anything? And blinking really hard felt like its only effect was starting the journey toward crow's feet.

The whole Weaver thing was currently lying somewhere on the borders between the Swamp of Frustration and the Evil Empire of Irritation. Her daddy would say 'widdled off', or something to that effect.

People were going to be relying on her to 'set the light free' whatever the heck that meant, yet everything that Sophie did seemed to be a reaction rather than some conscious effort and the weight of it all was starting to make her feel very small. If she didn't learn to control these powers what use would she be to Trancelvania?

A rustle came from one of the normal trees along the road but before Sophie could ask who was there an enormous creature all teeth and spikes and dampness dropped with a disagreeable plop to the ground in front of her. It was the kind of thing that looked like someone had asked an AI art generator to create a hand made of hate, but it couldn't quite decide where the drool should come from.

"Your money then your life," it hissed.

"Or your life," Sophie corrected, taking a step backward and considering that daylight really wasn't doing the thing any favours. Darkness would definitely have made it more aesthetically pleasing. In pitch black it would have looked amazing.

"Nope," the creature hissed, "it's a free market economy."

"That's not much of a negotiating tactic," she looked around her as she continued to back away from the steadily advancing creature, "there's not an awful lot in it for me."

"It's just a formality," it left a thick trail of slimy drool as it edged closer, "it's a buyer's market."

Suddenly there was something hard behind her and Sophie realised that the creature had backed her into a tree. Its greasy lips pulled into a sneer revealing silver teeth and it dribbled a bit more.

"Does a market not imply some kind of trade," Sophie looked around for anything with which to protect herself, or better still for some Weaver stuff to happen, "you know, goods and services?"

"I'm quite happy with exploitation."

"Why do you keep talking like that, are you one of those econometricists? My Mummy says those are bad."

It smiled with its mouth and slime as it raised insect-like arms and advanced on her in a way that didn't suggest cuddling.

She had nowhere to go now as the gooey insect creature was upon her, it smelled like old, wet socks.

From out of nowhere an acorn smacked off its long head and the creature jumped back in shock, it was used to having things thrown at it but usually out of an act of desperate self-defense.

"Who threw that?"

It snarled, looking left and right and the golden light above was making the slimy shell look like a rainbow going through an awkward phase.

Another acorn hit the monster under the chin. No, not another acorn, the same one?!

"Bug off, Dribbles!"

The little acorn hopped from twiggy foot to twiggy foot waving stubby little arms with fists raised like a boxer at a title fight and he had a voice like a cockney sparrow.

"Leave the lady alone or you'll have me to deal with."

The creature looked at the little acorn with what could either have been disgust or curiosity; it was hard to tell on a thing that was all teeth and no visible eyes. It lowered its head to bring its face right down to look at its erstwhile opponent.

"I don't see you being much of a barrier," a thick glob of slime oozed from its lips and landed with a splat next to the acorn.

"I've sorted bigger and uglier than you, mate," the acorn paused to think about that, "well, maybe not uglier."

"How very bullish," it tilted its head in curiosity, "but I think you'll find yourself over-extended."

"Bring it on," the acorn bounced on his feet, "float like a butterfly, sting like a Schwarzenegger."

The creature stretched out a long spiny finger and with a quick flick it pinged the acorn at Sophie, bouncing him off her forehead.

"Right," the acorn hoped up and down in rage, "I'll do you for that."

"No, you won't," Sophie had seen her fair share of bullies and discovering even Billy Brand had his fears had made her a lot less tolerant of them, "take a look around you, beastie, you see all this light coming from the trees that just appeared out of nowhere in Cuddleton."

Squaring up her shoulders and standing taller she took a step forward so that she was right under the creature's chin.

"Who do you think did that?"

Feeling even bolder she advanced again and this time the creature took a hesitant step back, no one had ever stood up to it before and it wasn't sure what to do in this situation. People were supposed to cower in terror and beg and stuff, they weren't supposed to give a load of lip, and definitely weren't supposed to point a finger in a threatening manner. This was unchartered territory and creature was starting to hear the sound incoming war drums.

"I did that," Sophie was feeling very bold of herself now, "do you know how I did it, beastie?"

The slimy insect creature was shrinking back faster than a politician in front of an open mic as Sophie marched steadily onward with finger raised like a gun under its chin.

"Because I," she put her foot down like a full stop the same way Mummy did when she meant that discussion was over, "I am a Weaver."

Beastie's spikes wilted and it straightened up like an obedient schoolboy, dropping its arms to its sides in a casual, offhand kind of way, trying to look as blasé as at all possible for something with the appearance of a demented fever dream about bugs in the plumbing.

"A Weaver, oh sorry, my mistake," it waved a hand indifferently, "this isn't the market for me. I'll just be off then. Post haste."

The beastie disappeared in a cartoonish puff of dust as it scarpered for the hills to rapidly rethink its life choices, a steady stream of drool forming unpleasant rainbows in the breeze.

"I could have taken him you know," the acorn looked up at her.

"I don't doubt that," Sophie knelt down to the acorn, "my way just meant that nobody would get hurt, including the monster of course."

"So, you're a Weaver," he said, "that's cool, I never thought that I'd actually get to meet one of you guys."

"It's a good thing that the beastie didn't ask me to prove it though, I haven't a clue how I've been doing all the hocus pocus."

"No idea?"

"Not a notion," she gave him a wink, "I'm Sophie."

"You must have confidence in spades then," the acorn looked across at the monster that was by now little more than a dark and unattractive smudge on the horizon, "I'm Brutus."

"Nice to meet you, Brutus," she looked left and right, "I don't suppose that you would be able to direct me to the nearest ruined city in roughly that direction?"

Brutus looked along the length of her finger and where it was pointing, then back at the Weaver, and then at her finger again.

"The city of Slumberg is that way, about a day on foot," he said at last, "but I'm pretty sure that it isn't a ruin, at least it wasn't the last time I was there."

"If it has a big wizard tower and lies that way then I'm pretty sure it is ruined now," she stood and checked that there were no more insect horrors hanging about, "I don't suppose you know a faster way to get there?"

"You're a Weaver," Brutus shrugged, "can't you just decide that you want to be there now and boom, wiggle of the nose and blink of an eye?"

"That's sort of how I got back here in the first place," Sophie gave her nose a test wiggle with her finger, "though really wanting it doesn't seem to be doing much for me. Mummy always said 'I want never gets', though I always thought that was just about sweets."

"Maybe click your heels and say there's no place like home?"

The acorn jumped onto her shoe then hopped up to grab her tunic and climb the strap of her satchel until he could sit on her shoulder, "I'm pretty sure I'm right about you deciding something and it happening, that's what all the stories say, you just need a bit of confidence that it will happen."

"I take it that you're coming with me to find Walker

then?"

"If he's a mate of yours then yes, you might need me to protect you along the way," he stuck out his chest and gave a smile that was somewhat adorable in its sincerity, "now click your heels and say let's be a stalker and go find Walker."

His self-confidence was endearing, if perhaps somewhat misplaced Sophie thought, thinking back to how many acorns she had seen defeated by a single determined crow and a roof tile.

She couldn't deny that she was feeling a bit taller about herself, seeing Billy Brand terrified of spiders was the emotional palate cleanser that she had needed and had given her enough nerve to stand up to an even worse bully, and it had run away like it was being chased by its own existential dread.

The image of Billy Brand out there now looking for a Weaver who was nowhere to be found gave her a smile, and if she worked out how to vanish again then she'd be pretty much untraceable to him.

Ha Billy Brand,

You've a face like a weasel,

I'll never be a prisoner,

Of the Shadow People.

Sophie laughed to herself and then blinked.

*

Daisy sniffed along the trail that Sophie had kicked for them on the edge of the forest of giant mushrooms. There was something of a bloodhound about the cow snuffling the ground, she wasn't going to give up or let it go for love nor money.

Up until the forest edge Sophie and the Shadow Person

had practically been walking in a line straight toward Walker and Daisy when suddenly they had changed course to skirt along the outside. Walker wasn't going to waste time thinking about it, he assumed that it was probably for the same reason that Daisy had turned her nose up at the mushrooms, fungus doesn't have the same easygoing nature as trees.

The trail wasn't particularly difficult for them to track though; it seemed that Sophie had taken every opportunity to kick stones and drag her feet. She was very clever for an eight year old.

Wikki spent most of the walk filling them in on what he had learned in the city from the Grand Magus. He glossed over the actual level of destruction in Slumberg in a manner similar to how local news reports about a drone strike on a small oil rich nation. He could only hope the ability to undo it all was within the Weaver's power.

Walker had been in a dark mood since learning about the Shadow Person having kidnapped Sophie. He blamed himself for it happening. It should have been him who jumped over the edge of the airship after her. He was supposed to be her guardian after all, he was the one who brought her here.

It was all a mix of feelings to his cogwheels. Legend said that the Shadow people were vampires, creatures of the night. After some long forgotten war they were driven into the desert lands beyond the Western Range, driven so far out that they could not safely make the journey back in even the longest of nights.

There were always rumours about one being spotted here or there, but usually that was all that they were. Rumours and secondhand stories. Truth was that nobody knew what started the conflict or why, or even if they were really driven out.

When rumours did bubble to the surface they were usually in the bogeyman kind of vein that mothers said to the children when they wanted five minutes of peace with the Blossom Hill.

And now the sun had been gone for days, there was nothing to stop them making their way back across the formerly scorching desert. And they could cross with an army.

Walker thought about the devastation Wikki said was in Slumberg. That was not the work of any army, and though he was loathe to admit the fact it also did not sound like the work of the Shadow People.

And these 'nightmares' were something else entirely, and it sounded like this had happened before the Long Night.

So then why was the ruin of Slumberg not more widely known throughout Trancelvania?

His reverie was broken when Daisy came to a sudden stop and stood perfectly still with her head alert.

"What is it girl?"

Drawing his cutlass Walker put one finger to Wikki's lips in a hint to shut up and then stepped up beside Daisy.

They had come upon a dusty path leading into a darkened valley, and Sophie's not so subtle trail seemed to be going into it.

Stepping quietly Walker followed the scuff marks along the path and all the way up to an old gnarled tree.

Here the trail looked strange. There was shuffled stone as if someone had sat down; a few feet away a real mess of panicked footprints; a load of strange dotted marks; and there were needle-like lying hairs everywhere.

The panicked set of footprints looked to have ran off into the valley followed by a trail of the hairs.

Something had scared off one of the pair and the other seemed to have vanished as there was no trail leading away from where the person had sat, other than a length of cut rope.

"Urticating hairs," Wikki came alongside Walker, (p85 of C.P. Crawley's *Things that Crawl on your Face at Night*) "some tarantulas throw them as a defence mechanism, though I don't know of any spiders whose size matches those prints on the ground."

"Spiders," Walker looked at the trail of hair and the shuffling of feet, "Sophie met a moody spider outside of Cuddleton. Could she somehow have summoned it and made it bigger to scare off the Shadow Person?"

"She's the Weaver," Wikki opened his pages to the more or less blank section entitled 'Weaver', "in theory she can do anything that she wants."

"There is no sign where she and the spider went," Walker looked up and down the path, "she must have transported them somewhere. Maybe back to Cuddleton, maybe somewhere else."

"There's no way to tell," Wikki looked from Daisy to Walker, "Weavers aren't bound by the laws of our universe."

That was a problem. Weavers were about as easy to track as an imaginary friend. And without Sophie their quest had come to a standstill. Or more to the point, without Sophie they *had* no quest.

"Come on," Walker hefted his cutlass and started marching, "we will keep on the trail, the Shadow Person will not have given up so easily."

10..

A BATTLE OF WITS

"Me and my big mouth," Sophie said as she tried to force the bars of her cell in the dungeon.

She had tried every rhyme that she could imagine, including some using words that she definitely wouldn't want Daddy to know that she had been repeating. After that she had tried wishing hard, and then had tried wishing really hard. None of it had worked so now she was trying the age old tactic of brute force and ignorance.

This Weaver business was becoming more hassle than it was worth. One wrong thought and she had landed herself in the middle of a cell in a cold and dark dungeon, with light coming only from a lantern in the corridor outside. There were chains hanging from the ceiling for some reason and there was a constant drip-drip-drip of water.

Sophie seemed to be the only person currently a guest of this establishment at the moment. Brutus didn't count because he was so small from his perspective the bars were more like decorative columns, and as such he had taken to exploring the room.

"Yep," he said after giving it a few minutes of thorough assessment, "it's a dungeon alright."

"Uh huh," Sophie kicked at the lock of her cell, to no effect.

"Doesn't look like it has been used in a while," Brutus was examining the lock of one of the other cells and it looked to have seized from disuse. He examined the lock of Sophie's cell and seeing it was the same he gave it a test kick. Then a test tug. Then a test strain. And then he decided to sit down before he gave himself a test hernia.

"Well, that settles it," he wiped a bead of sap from his brow, "if I can't shift it then you've no hope. Might as well settle in for the long haul. You know any sing-a-longs?"

The air was dry in the room which Sophie thought odd until she noticed that the drip-dripping was falling into a drain. A dungeon just wasn't a proper dungeon without dripping water, but clearly the designers were worried about mould so stuck a drain below the aesthetic drip.

Sophie took a moment to appreciate the conscientiousness of the design, and then she kicked the bars again.

"HELP!"

If all else fails scream the house down, that usually worked at home.

"Somebody help me," she shouted toward the door with the light outside, "I'm trapped in a torture chamber and I can't get out!"

"Just a thought," Brutus dandered back into the cell, "are you sure that you want to be drawing the torturer into the torture chamber?"

"From the look of the place it hasn't had anyone to torture for some time," Sophie started kicking the bars for attention, "they've maybe grown out of pain and suffering."

"All the more reason not to attract someone who might feel that they need the practice."

Just then the room was plunged into darkness as an enormous shadow blotted out the tiny barred window in the door. It made a few confused grunts before walking off again, letting lantern light spill back in.

"Hey," Sophie called after it, "come back!"

"Huh?"

The shadow reappeared before the window and plunged the room back into darkness. It made some confused grunts but couldn't see anything so walked off again.

"Oh for the love of blarney," Sophie started kicking the bars again, "hey dopey, I don't disappear just because the lights go out."

Her mummy said the same thing about the mess in her bedroom.

The room once again plunged into darkness and this time she kept kicking the bars.

A voice as slow as glaciers, in several respects, spoke, "Is someone there?"

"Yes," bang-bang-rattle-bang.

She heard a key turn in the lock, and with a groan of old and unused hinges the door rumbled open but no light entered the room. The enormous shadow completely filled the doorway.

"Are you sure?"

"Pretty certain," Sophie's expression was what's commonly known as the 'Confused Kermit'.

With a few awkward twists and ducking under the doorframe the huge bulk was able to squeeze its way in, followed by the warming flow of lantern light.

The creature was for all intents and purposes a blob of muscle with a belly; ostensibly man shaped and shrouded head to foot in robes of fashionable 'Executioners Black', with a voice as dark as chocolate covered coal.

"How did you get in here?"

"That would take a long time to explain."

"You aren't supposed to be in here."

"I know that," Sophie tried to smile innocently, as most prisoners might, "would you be able to let me out please?"

"I can't let you out until I know why you're in there," the bulk of muscle looked at Sophie then the door and then at Sophie again, "I need to speak to my supervisor."

"What? Why? Just let me out. You already said that I'm not supposed to be in here."

"You are not supposed to be in there but you are in there and I can't let you out until I know why you are in there because there is not supposed to be anyone in there but you are in there."

The bulk of muscle sat down on a stool in the corner, "My head hurts."

"Let's just start again, shall we?" Sophie could feel the Dungeon Keeper's mental faculties straining like a guitar string from across the room, "Where exactly am I?"

"In the old dungeon," the Dungeon Keeper brushed back his hood to reveal a black leather executioner's mask underneath. He scratched the top of it.

"Yes," Sophie let a breath out through gritted teeth, "but where is this dungeon?"

"In the prison," he said in a way that sounded like he was really hoping that he was being helpful.

Pressing her head against the cell bars in frustration Sophie wondered if that leather mask had cut off all circulation to the Dungeon Keeper's brain. It looked tight enough.

"Where is the prison," she took a measured breath, "what is the name of the city?"

"This is the city of Paris'Häl," the Dungeon Keeper smiled... well, the mask twitched around the mouth, "jewel of the Crystal Desert and capitol of the Free Lands of Shadow."

"Free Lands of Shadow, so would you say the people might call themselves Shadow People," Sophie blinked her eyes rapidly hoping to zap anywhere, "oh bum."

"Is there something wrong with your eyes?"

*

A frost was starting to settle into the dry gorge that Walker and the others were making their way through. The imposed night had been getting colder, there was no denying it now. The gang had less time than Walker thought when he had originally been sent forth by the Oracowl.

The trail that had been left by the Shadow Person was relatively straightforward to follow; a lot of panicked running from the spider attack followed by a timid loop back to the old tree and then a resigned trudging through this gorge that ran more or less parallel to the forest of mushrooms.

This dusty path had about as much vibrancy as a party political broadcast. There was little to no vegetation and they had seen nothing in the way of animal life. It was almost as if this place had embraced the concept of inhospitability, which was odd given that just over the hill to the left was a forest of mushrooms beyond the dreams of even the most enthusiastic free spirit.

Wikki had spotted some other unusual prints in the dusty

floor and had ran on ahead to investigate against the vocal and largely pointless protesting of Walker. The excitable book didn't possess much in the way of common sense but rather an insatiable curiosity that overrode anything as mundane as a survival instinct. Clearly he didn't have any entries about cats.

"I guess we will call him a scout," Walker glanced absently at Daisy, "and if we see a camp fire up ahead we will know that he found the Shadow Person."

"Moo," said Daisy, sniffing the ground and continuing at her unrelenting pace.

"Guys!"

"Holy moly," Walker's springs instinctively sprung as Wikki popped out of nowhere.

"Oops, sorry," the Tome sidled up to his companions, "I found out what the trail is, we're on an Inurning Path."

"A what?"

"Moo?"

"An Inurning Path," Wikki explained, "when some animals know that they are going to die they follow these paths to a peaceful resting place. Like an Elephant's Graveyard."

"Are we going to see something gruesome up ahead?"

"Well," Wikki waved a spindly hand in the air, "there's a griffon around the corner who is none too good, but a group of Djellohs have arrived to make it comfortable."

Djellohs are a creature that warrants some description. Sophie had spied a pair in the Inn of the Counting Sheep, not technically individual beings but each a walking colony of cells much like a jellyfish. The cells worked together with a hive mind which meant that they had a bit more intellectual capacity than seaweed, unlike jellyfish, and also unlike jellyfish they didn't go around stinging strangers. They smelled oddly similar to strawberry.

They are a strictly vegetarian species, having evolved from a family of amoeba who had settled in a jam factory and rather enjoyed the aesthetic.

Somewhere in their cultural evolution they took on the trait of tending to the dead and dying of other species in the same way that some yoghurts had cultures that liked to live in your gut. The hanging around the dead and dying thing made Walker think that they were a bit morbid. Though he had to admit that he would be a vegetarian too if he had to work with bodies all day.

"Were you talking to them," Walker started forward again, "did they see the Shadow Person?"

"They haven't seen anyone on their journey," Wikki fell in step alongside Daisy, "however the path forks to the left just around the corner, it looks like our assailant might have went that way."

"That is toward the Cracked Vale," Walker looked back at his travelling companions, "the only thing beyond there is the Castle of Pandemonium."

"I... don't know what that is," Wikki looked confused and his pages fluttered, "I don't have a single entry in me about that. How do I not even have a footnote about that?"

"Because it is Pandemonium," Walker lowered his head, hefted his sword and started walking.

"Moo," said Daisy, starting after the clockwork man.

"You know that isn't helpful," Wikki said to the backs of his companions, before trotting off after them. He did not like having gaps in his knowledge, missing entries or outdated information made tomes useless, just ask any encyclopedia printed just before 26 December 1991.

"Because it's Pandemonium," he mumbled as he mentally began the new entry, "what kind of explanation is that?!"

*

"No no no," Sophie rested her head on the cell bars in frustration, "I was not sent here, I blinked and then I arrived here."

"So you are here for a reason then," the Dungeon Keeper sat up and Sophie imagined that he was smiling as the gears had started to turn at last, "to arrive you had to have been sent."

"I was not sent," she slid to the floor, the gears were grinding, "I did it myself."

"Ah ha, you see, you sent you," the Dungeon Keeper crossed his arms smugly, "what did you do that you sent you here?"

"I. Did not. Do. Anything," oh my word she thought as she stared at the floor, he is profoundly thick, "this was. An. Accident."

"But then how did you get here?"

The Dungeon Keeper continued to question her with the resolute and indefatigable logic that if she was in a prison cell then she must have done something to get there. And it had to have been something pretty bad as his people no longer actually used dungeons and she was in a room that was for all intents and purposes decorative.

For Sophie's part the last thing she wanted to reveal to the Shadow People was her nature as a Weaver. She still had no idea what that actually meant beyond possibly 'my own biggest inconvenience'.

"Why don't you just tell him the truth," Brutus was bored watching the Dungeon Keeper battle and lose to his own wits and stepped into sight, casting a wink at Sophie, "that a wizard was getting a bit too fresh in the tavern, you bopped him in his mana stones and accidentally got portalled here."

"Uh yeah, that was it exactly," Sophie didn't know what any of that actually meant but she looked up at those big open eyes hidden under the leather mask and gave what can only be described as the least convincing smile in the history of false smiles, honestly, it was one for the record books. She hammered the point home with a weak thumbs up.

"Why is that acorn talking?"

"Excuse me for having an education, chum," Brutus stuck what passed for his chest out, "after a workout some of us read more than just the instructions on the back of a jar of steroids."

The Dungeon Keeper stood and extended to as full a height as the room would allow and tromped up to the cell until his shadow loomed over them like a Tyrannosaur looking at a snack.

"I do not use steroids," the mass of muscle growled, "little man."

"Who are you calling little?!"

"You-"

"Enough, the pair of you," Sophie's patience had frayed and they had just pulled on the last thread, "Brutus sit down and be quiet, and you, open this door and let me out of here or find someone who will."

Arms ramrod straight, fists clenched and nostrils flared Sophie felt every inch like Mummy when Daddy came home late and 'dopey'. Brutus sat his backside down immediately and the enormous Dungeon Keeper froze in fear; nothing in the world is more terrifying than a woman on the warpath.

"Well," she transferred her hands to her hips, "what are you waiting for?"

"I don't have a key," the huge hooded man was shaking with the onset of a massive panic attack.

"Well," Sophie kept her voice level, "go and get one."

"Yes, miss."

The Dungeon Keeper bolted for the door without trying to duck through and immediately got himself wedged in the frame by the shoulders like some kind of cartoon idiot.

"Uh-oh."

He puffed and he groaned, and so did the doorframe. His feet spun on the ground kicking up a small cloud of dust as he tried to push through. He managed to squeeze one arm through the door and was trying to pull himself the rest of the way.

Brutus was about to offer help when there came a pop like a champagne cork, at which point the Dungeon Keeper's britches split and he shot forward and knocked himself out on a lantern.

"Good grief," Sophie sat on a nearby stool and contemplated the benefits of paying attention in school.

"What in the stars is that racket?"

A muffled but matronly voice came from somewhere in the corridor followed by the clunk of a latch and creak of hinges moving a heavy door, and then light footsteps of expensive sounding shoes.

"Joh'Naffan, the door again?"

The Dungeon Keeper for his part answered by remaining unconscious and face down on the floor.

A shadow appeared over the fallen mass of muscle, it had a feminine form and wore long black robes that flowed along her slender body and a black veil over her head. This must have been the supervisor that the Dungeon Keeper had mentioned almost a chapter ago.

"What are you doing down here anyway, you big oaf?"

She knelt by his side to give him a few gentle pats on the cheek to rouse him, Sophie reckoned that it would probably take something far harder to knock some sense into the dolt.

"He was trying to work out why I was in here," Sophie called over and the supervisor turned toward the darkened cells in surprise, "so that he could let me out."

The supervisor rose elegantly and walked with the dignity and grace of one used to people being deferential in her general direction.

With a clap of her hands the lanterns around the dungeon all sparked to life and the supervisor regarded the young lady in the green tunic before her.

"It is perhaps a good question," she had intense green eyes that seemed to glow from within the black veil, "these dungeons have been closed to the public for decades, why are you in here?"

"At the risk of repeating history, it was an accident," she was having visions of running through all this rubbish again, "I blinked and I was in here."

The supervisor tilted her head to one side and pushed back her veil. Her hair was grey but there were hints of a vibrant red still dotted through it, she had long and slender features and the complexion of one who probably inherited a yacht at some point. She also had the look of someone who did a lot of thinking in her free time.

"Come with me, child," she clicked her fingers and the doors of all the cells swung open with a series of rusty squeaks, "the dungeon is no place for a Weaver."

11.

A RAT'S TRAP

The Cracked Vale existed in a kind of crossroads in time and space like queuing in the post office and that depending on your perspective was either beautiful or terrible, and sticking with the post office analogy the smell would be depending on whether or not the person in front of you had eaten spicy food the night before.

Walker and the group stood on the crest of a hill overlooking a huge stretch of barren land that was fractured and broken. From within those cracks came a vicious red glow and chimneys of acrid, black smoke.

Not long ago this had been rolling green fields with a crystal clear river serenely snaking through it and yet it had at the very same time for millennia been a devastated hellscape. It was a nightmare for map makers. Going back to the original statement it wasn't so much a crossroads in time and space as a spaghetti junction, with all the unintended horror that comes with the commuting equivalent of blood splatter analysis.

Wikki protested that it wasn't meant to be this way at all.

His records spoke of the green fields, the blue river, and on the other side of the vale was the capitol city with the beautiful spires of the Royal Palace. Whatever corruption had caused this was also starting to affect him as he could no longer recall the name of the Capitol, and when he turned to the page the entry was an indistinct blur. Paper doesn't refuse ink, but sometimes ink can be unreliable in what information it shares.

It was frustrating to say the least. Personally he blamed that weird looking black void with the swirling purple mist hanging off in the distance, it didn't look like it belonged here.

"I am guessing that is where our nightmares have come from," Walker said what everybody had been thinking, "now how do we close it?"

"Moo," offered Daisy.

"I don't know if even Sophie will be able to do that," Wikki said, "not by herself. The darkness within is unlike anything I've ever seen, that void is not just an absence of light, it's like it's trying to swallow up all light. Like an extremely picky black hole."

"She has created light before," Walker looked across the broken fields, trying to find the path of the Shadow Person, "but I agree, I do not know if it will be enough."

"Moo," Daisy tramped a foot with determination.

"Daisy's right," Wikki bounced with renewed vigour and opened himself to a page that said 'Hackneyed Epiphany', "that's why we're here, we'll help her find the light."

"Come on," Walker saw a shadow trudging in the distance broodily yet thematically appropriately lit by the underground fires, "we have got a villain to catch."

*

Sophie walked through the dusty corridor from the cell trying to keep herself a step behind the supervisor without looking like she was trying to keep herself a step behind the supervisor.

She had to correct herself, the lady was not a supervisor, she was Ayri'Elle, Duchess of the Coh'Penagon family of the Free Lands.

It was quite a mouthful, and being that she was a Shadow Person it was a mouthful that also left a sour taste.

Joh'Naffan, the Dungeon Keeper had went back to whatever other duties a man of such massive proportions and unique intellect might have to perform. In this case it was to unblock the loos, but he wasn't telling anybody that.

"I'm surprised to find a Weaver in Paris'Häl," her ladyship spoke conversationally in a way that Sophie found quite disarming, "the Free Lands are awfully far out of the way from Trancelvania, and we have little if any dealings with them. It keeps the trouble from our door."

"What would make you think that I am a Weaver?" She tried a feint, "I'm just a really bad wizard."

"Wizards are all men, my dear," the Duchess said, "the patriarchal society of Trancelvania would never allow a woman to train as a wizard, and certainly not a girl. What age are you, really?"

"Eight," Sophie felt small and cornered and it made the High Lady appear all the more grand, "and I really don't know what I am doing."

"It's alright, child," Ayri'Elle turned to Sophie and gave her a look of almost motherly concern, "you are quite safe here, the Free Lands are a haven for all those with gifts."

"I was kidnapped by a Shadow Person," Sophie didn't feel

afraid of the Duchess, in a way she was a bit like her grandmother, with more lace and fewer boiled sweets.

"You mean the mercenaries who use our name to inspire fear," the Lady's face darkened slightly, "violent exiles trading off the memory of a long forgotten conflict from when we chose to leave Trancelvania. They are not our people, but we have been trying to undo the damage they have caused in our name."

Violent exiles? That was not something Sophie had expected to hear, although having seen Billy Brand being sent to the principal's office on more than one occasion it was not entirely a surprise.

"So the people here..?"

"Are for the most part a peaceful collective of thinkers, explorers, and magii," the Duchess turned the handle on the door at the end of the corridor that opened into a vast promenade of sandy stone and brightly lit by lanterns. "We have no interest in interfering with the Kingdom of Trancelvania."

Sophie was awestruck as the vast expanse of the city that opened up before her.

The dungeons appeared to be three or four storeys up as part of an enormous pyramid-shaped building that Ayri'Elle explained was the central court and administrative centre. It had a flat top and huge sandstone bridges radiated out from it like the points of a star to the faraway walls of the city, from overhead the whole city would look like a sliced orange. Beneath these viaducts the city was built in concentric circles with a countless number of towers, domes, and smaller flat topped pyramids, and between each circle was a calm flow of water.

Huge stone bridges curled out into the various districts

from the viaducts and there were huge rope elevators that seemed to be steam powered for lifting heavy cargo from the ships docked in the canals.

And lanterns blazed everywhere giving the sandstone a warm glow of a summer day that was full of life.

The Duchess led the way from the promenade onto the viaduct before them and explained how the city was divided into different districts devoted to the arts, sciences, philosophy and religion, academia and guildhalls in the inner rings. The outer ring held industry, the trade marketplace, warehousing, and the military.

As she looked over the walls Sophie was amazed by how much life she could see, people were everywhere going about their business. And everything was so organised, so well laid out; back home city design meant if there was a gap jam a building into it and find out who owed tax on it.

"This city is amazing," she said at last, before looking up at the stars and her eyes being caught by something else, "oh wow."

Enormous towers stood around the walls of the city and here and there within the grounds, each was crowned with some kind of bulb that looked like a lily whose petals were yet to open.

"The Paris'Häl lilies, a plant which blooms in the sun and closes up at night, we replicated the design and they are from which the city takes its name," Ayri'Elle explained, "during the day the towers open out to shelter the city from the desert sun."

"But why?" Sophie vaguely remembered Joh'Naffan saying something about the jewel of the Crystal Desert.

"Did you not notice that we are all pale skinned and red haired?"

"Now that you mention it..." she trailed off, she had thought something was peculiar but hadn't quite been able to put her finger on it. But yes, every single person walking by her was red haired.

"Ginger people in the desert," she looked to the Duchess, "I can see why you would need the shelter. But how could everybody be ginger, surely even by the law of averages there should be one or two blondes or a brunette?"

"It's the power that gives us the red hair and pale skin," Ayri'Elle had the look of one about to unburden herself and at the same time knowing that she was going to have to do a lot of explaining. Having an awkward silence that felt far longer than it probably was prompted her to just spit it out, "The red hair and pale skin that burns in sunlight is how natural magic users got the name Vam'Pyres."

Sophie felt the need to go to the bathroom again.

*

There was a tremendous heat in the Cracked Vale that caused the landscape all around to shimmer in the light of the fires.

Walker worried about Daisy, she was the only one of the group who actually needed water, but that was something they did not have and it was doubtless they would find it in these burning fields.

Of course if the ever faithful cow was feeling any discomfort she was keeping it to herself. She marched stoically across the hard and scorched ground keeping her eyes on the direction they had seen the Shadow Person heading.

"It really stinks here," he waved his hand in front of his pointy nose, which had the effect of creating an airflow that carried more of the rotten egg smell to him, "did one of you drop a silent one?"

"That's brimstone," Wikki said offhandedly, "sulphur fumes from the volcanic fissures. We're probably walking through a cocktail of gases."

"That could not be healthy," Walker looked ahead at Daisy, and then at Wikki. Being metal and clockwork he didn't breathe so poison gas was not a problem for him, but the others were in danger.

"In the short term we will be fine," Wikki stopped Walker with an earnest hand on his arm, "but you are at the most risk. Volcanic gases can be corrosive and your cooling systems will be circulating it around your body. Not to mention that heat causes metal to expand..."

"Are you worried that I might pop my cogs?"

"Short answer, yes," Wikki looked over at Daisy who had now stopped to look on, "maybe you should shut yourself down until we get across the Vale, let Daisy carry you."

Walker looked at the faithful cow and then across the shimmering plain bathed in the red glow from within the earth, and then at the stars overhead who seemed to be watching the gang with hope.

He didn't want to be a burden to them, not when they had so much to do and so far to travel, and no water to quench Daisy's thirst. And there was the matter of the Shadow Person they were pursuing, Wikki was foolhardy enough to plunge headlong into a fight but he had the combat ability of, well, a book.

"I will be alright," Walker started forward once more, his face set into a look of grim determination, "I have enough spare parts stowed to keep me off the scrap heap."

In his head he added 'I hope'.

The corrosive gas would threaten his springs the most, they were fine metal and wound tight, it wouldn't take much wear for them to snap, and then he wouldn't be able to move.

Heat was a greater risk than the gas though; the cogs in his body would be fine and would be easily fixed, but it would take just one cog popping in his logic engine and that would be it over, he'd simply stop. They were all so small and tightly packed together that no one here would be able to reassemble them. One cog in his head and no more Walker.

'I am not going to burden them' he said to himself as he inhaled another breath and felt his cooling fans spread it through him. At the same time he felt a small spring snap and he lost the use of his pinkie finger, he hoped that there wouldn't be much more.

Standing tall he marched on, passing Daisy who looked back to Wikki with a questioning moo. The Tome admired the clockwork man's determination, and he knew that it was largely because he was unfairly taking the blame for losing Sophie. His machine logic in action, he had a task to complete but had failed in a function and his system could not reconcile the error, a mechanical reproduction of guilt.

"Walker," he said as he and Daisy caught up, "we'll find her."

The ground cracked without warning and suddenly the gang tumbled into a hot and dark pit, and everyone landed on Wikki with a series of 'oofs'.

The walls were smooth and glassy, almost as if they had been cut with some sort of plasma.

Or fire magic!

A small landslide of pebbles clattered down the wall

behind the fallen trio and their eyes turned as one.

A figure stood on the edge of the pit in clothing so black that it seemed to absorb all the light around, and he held in his hand a glowing red mana stone.

"I was wondering what was taking you so long, you've only been following me since that tree," Billy Brand pulled back his hood revealing his red hair and rat face, his eyes and crooked teeth glowed menacingly like an oncoming train in the light of the magic stone.

"I'm sure Stinky Sophie won't be far behind now that I have her friends," he cast a silver thread that whipped out by itself to bind the gang by one leg each, "let's throw a surprise party for her in the Castle of Pandemonium."

12

A TOP SHELF BOOK

"I recognise that look," Ayri'Elle said as Sophie took a step back after the Duchess revealed that she and everyone else in the city were Vam'Pyres.

"Would it comfort you if I said that the bloodsucking thing is a myth?"

"It would help," Sophie tried blinking rapidly on the off-chance that she might suddenly find herself somewhere that felt safer, like a lion enclosure.

"It is a myth," Ayri'Elle smiled and stepped to the edge of the viaduct, "blood has about the same nutritional value as a nail. The whole thing is a slur from the early days before we left Trancelvania."

She leaned on the wall and looked down upon the wide canal that separated the circular districts from the main pyramid. This happened so often, people got caught up so much in myth and hearsay that they forget to think or examine things and draw their own conclusions.

"The old kings of Trancelvania could not abide natural magic in man or woman, but the magic is in our blood regardless and the perversion of that simple truth is the root of the myth," the Duchess looked upon the people in the city below, "and that is what led to the conflict between our peoples and why we crossed the desert to start free. In the patriarchy of Trancelvania only a man can be a scholar, own a business, rule the land, or Gods forbid use magic."

Sophie tilted her head as she watched the Duchess, the lady did not sound angry or resentful, just deeply sad. But looking around this fantastic city her people had done remarkably well despite past adversity. They had built and prospered in a place where five minutes out of the shade would leave them looking like a packet of wafer thin ham.

"For what it might be worth that doesn't sound an awful lot like the Kingdom I just came from," Sophie stood next to Ayri'Elle to look out over the city, "Cuddleton was just a lovely wee country town, and when I looked into the mana well in the Tower of the Grand Magus it showed him talking to the Queen."

"Queen?" The Duchess gave Sophie a look of genuine surprise. She had not been expecting to hear that, but then the people of Paris'Häl had been effectively cut off from the Kingdom for a long time, maybe they were finally starting to collectively grow up.

"Yeah," Sophie leaned on the warm stone wall of the viaduct and stared out over the city and at nothing in particular, all the people down there going about their lives and the real tragedy began to sink in, "I saw her with him right before the nightmares came and made him destroy the city."

"What are these nightmares?"

Sophie did her best to explain what she had seen in the

ruin of Slumberg and in the mana well as the ghost of the Grand Magus walked alone in the tower oblivious to the ruin all around him.

Walking side by side along the viaduct the Duchess listened in quiet contemplation as the Weaver explained the porcelain faced creatures that had driven the Magus to wipe out the city. Sophie said that the Queen and the Magus seemed to think the nightmares came from some sort of void or portal over a castle.

Brutus sat in one of her pockets listening on and hoping that no one had forgotten about him. The Duchess Ayri'Elle had paid him little heed, in her world of inherited magic a talking acorn was as normal as sliced white bread, and meaning no disrespect to Brutus as mundane as sliced white bread.

He couldn't make heads or tails of all this talk about nightmares and voids, it all sounded very Freudian. At least when the conversation turned to the Purse Loyal who kidnapped Sophie there became a definite target that Brutus could punch.

"Just who was the Purse Loyal," Ayri'Elle paused on the viaduct once more, they had walked far along the broad thoroughfare with its lanterns burning over the city and were nearing the first of the canals between the ringed districts, "the one who kidnapped you?"

"Billy Brand," Sophie said the name with less anger than usual, she found herself fearing him less and less, "he's a cheeky snot from my school."

"Bih'Librand," the Duchess recognised the name instantly, "the Librands are something of a nuisance. They wanted us to invade and conquer Trancelvania, and were exiled after they attempted to stage a coup in Paris'Häl. They are an unpleasant caste of scoundrels."

"That sounds about right."

"Unfortunately now if what you say is true we may have to do exactly what they wanted and send our army across the Crystal Desert."

"What? Why?"

"If these nightmares are as you say then we have to destroy their base before they can threaten Paris'Häl," the Duchess did not look at Sophie, "which means we'll have to capture the outlying territories first to contain the nightmare forces."

"But, that will be war," Sophie didn't know what to say, "the Kingdom is in shambles. It's just farmers and folk, there was no sign of any army."

"Then with any luck they will surrender without a fight and we will be able to move on the nightmares."

"But… but people don't like to be invaded, that's one thing that I definitely took away from history class, they won't just let you walk in and stick a flag down."

"Our army is far larger, and we are all magii," Ayri'Elle leaned on the wall of the viaduct, "believe me I don't wish for there to be conflict with Trancelvania, but if it comes to a fight it will be over quickly."

"There has to be another way," she pleaded with the Duchess, "Trancelvania is a victim in this, they aren't an enemy."

Ayri'Elle turned to the young woman, her eyes were sad but showed great strength of will that told Sophie that she would do what she must to protect these lands, even at the expense of her neighbours.

"The only alternative," the Duchess said at last, "is if the Weaver can somehow destroy or drive out the nightmares before our forces cross the desert. Sophie, trust me when I say that is the outcome that I would prefer."

"Me? But I don't know how to do any of this? I can't."

"You will have to learn, and quickly too," the Duchess turned her eyes to the faraway city walls and the desert beyond, "tonight the desert is going to see its first frost in aeons, our army will have to cross before the frost turns to snow. When winter comes it will be too late, for everyone."

"But I don't know how?" Sophie was starting to feel tiny, caught between a rock and a hard place, or a rock and a hardened face.

"You do, my dear," the Duchess turned to her, "you just don't know it yet. We will do what we can, what we must, but you may be the only one with the power to really change anything."

"You can't leave this fate to me," Sophie was more panicked now than when Walker first told her of his quest in Cuddleton and as if on cue thunder cracked overhead, "you can't. I don't know how."

She could feel the weight of the world upon her and right now she felt every bit the eight year old that she actually was. Tiny. Insignificant.

The Duchess seemed to be getting bigger, looming over her, becoming more menacingly adult, and Sophie by contrast could feel herself getting smaller, more awkward, frightened, and suddenly very alone in the world.

She turned to run away from it all. And then she blinked.

*

Standing in a courtyard that looked as though it were made of black stone that had melted and congealed against the really sinister tower that stood before them the trio of adventurers knew that they were up a certain creak without a paddle.

"Any thoughts," Walker whispered to Wikki, "what is to happen next?"

"Haven't a clue," the Tome stared up the dizzying height of the black tower framed against the purple vortex, "I think that we've probably found the bad guys."

"You would be right, Tome," another book was walking down the twisted black stairwell from the tower; it had a cracked black leather cover with rusted metal book corners, silver writing in some forgotten language on its face and it was wrapped in a silver chain and sealed with leather straps.

It was a Grimoire. Wikki couldn't believe it, those evil books were all supposed to have been banished back to the demonic realm from whence they had come. And it had taken a lot of banishing.

"Purse Loyal," the Grimoire turned its attention to their captor, "why have you brought these beings to Pandemonium?"

Before Billy Brand could answer there came a strange whispering on the wind, several quiet voices all speaking at once in snakelike tones and looking up he saw four dark forms circling around the tower and spiraling down toward the gang.

"Now that's something you don't see every day," Wikki commented as the black creatures swirled through the air leaving smoky trails in their wake. He knew of no creature that fitted the description of these beings and that horrified him more than their expressionless porcelain faces and empty black eyes.

They circled like flies, inspecting everyone, each one

staring in turn and never stopping in their flight.

"Clockwork."

"Paper."

"Burger."

Their whispering voices were fast but emotionless.

"Companions of the Weaver."

"You brought them here."

"Why have you brought them?"

"They should not be here."

"The Weaver," Billy Brand said as he tried to work out which of these beings he should be talking to, "she escaped from me, but she will come for her friends."

"She will come here."

"We cannot allow this."

"She must not come here."

"You are a fool, Purse Loyal."

"Foolish boy."

"She was to go to the Pits of Flame."

"She must go to the Pits of Flame."

"To be put to flame."

"It is too late."

"Where they go she will follow."

"She doesn't know what she is doing," Billy Brand pleaded for attention, "let me set a trap and I will catch her again."

"Pathetic boy."

"She will learn."

"You have imperiled us."

"We must adjust to survive."

Walker watched the creatures, the nightmare things were like clouds with doll faces, always circling and whispering dark words, they had no real form that he could see. Insidious was the word he was looking for.

They drifted around this courtyard of a corrupted fortress of doom as a cold air drifted in from the growing night and ignoring the protests of the Shadow Person.

"Mechanical man."

"The one who brought the Weaver."

"Overheated from the Cracked Vale."

"Corroded from the air."

"Cooling in the night."

"Nothing but parts."

"Wants to be a hero."

"Pathetic ticking of clockwork."

"Another fool."

"Heroes die."

One of the nightmares drifted right up to Walker and with empty eyes it stared right into him.

"Some heat in the heart."

A twang that was more like a bang came from within Walker's chest, his eyes had a moment of shock and he coughed up a mouthful of blue liquid coolant, the nightmare had heated him until his primary spring had snapped and the energy of the coil exploded in his chest.

"Walker," Wikki screamed and rushed to grab the clockwork man as in slow motion he fell lifeless to the ground, frozen in shape with only darkness in his eyes and coolant leaking from his body.

"Dispose of them."

"Put them with the others."

"We can use them in the void."

"Summon the army."

"Bring all the darkness."

"Purse Loyal you will fight."

"You will fight or you will join the void."

"This is your penance."

"Do not fail again."

With their warning given and lesson taught the nightmares took to the air once more, circling the length of the tower high above the assembly until they were swallowed by the darkness somewhere in the swirling void.

"Walker," Wikki cradled his fallen companion and Daisy looked over his shoulder, a tear forming in her eye.

"Right," the Grimoire said from the steps, summoning two hulking brutes who were bare chested and wearing faceless iron masks, "throw the book and that scrap in the dungeon, they can go to the void with everyone we don't use."

"What about the cow?" Billy Brand said weakly, until now the thought had never occurred that he was one of the bad guys, he just figured that he was making his way in the world, like a dashing rogue or something.

"Lock her in a stable," the Grimoire started back up the stairs with a dismissive wave, "we'll find something to feed her to."

THE SECRET QUEEN

Crystals of frost had formed along the endless sea of sand dunes and made a crisp crunch under Sophie's feet as she ran away from her troubles. Suddenly appearing out in the desert had not caused the same shock as her previous blinks, she had wanted to be far away from the problems growing ever larger around her and for once the powers had manifested as she wanted.

The city of Paris'Häl was no more than a glowing smudge on the horizon behind her. A huge glowing smudge it had to be said, but a smudge nonetheless. An amazing city existing in the most unlikely of places, built far away from the troubles of the world.

But not far enough it seemed. And now they were going to send an army to sort out the problems of Trancelvania unless Sophie could save it first. It was like putting out a fire by blowing up a dam, yes technically it would douse the flames but ultimately it's going to create more problems than it'll solve.

Pulling her cloak tighter against the cold she put her head

down and tried to fight back tears. What was she supposed to do?

The nightmares were unlike anything that she had seen before and were clearly a powerful force. What was a lost eight year old girl supposed to do against things like them? Where was she even supposed to find them, let alone fight them? Billy Brand had said something about the Pits of Flame, but that didn't mean any more to her than Timbuktu. It was just a name of a place that she'd never seen.

Why should it be her problem anyway? She never asked for this responsibility. It was Walker who had brought her here, and he didn't even know what he was bringing her here to do.

Anger was beginning to build in Sophie. Walker had brought her here and he was supposed to be her guardian, but where was he? He didn't even try to save her on the airship and he obviously was not in any hurry to get back to her when they crashed.

Walker had brought her here and then abandoned her to fight these monsters by herself.

Not just monsters, also stop an army that was preparing to invade the Kingdom, and of course prevent the end of the world. It was too much to ask of an eight year old with a runny nose.

And the army might already be on the march. The Duchess Ayri'Elle had said that they would need to cross the desert before the snow came.

Tiredness was starting to set in as her little feet sank into the cold sand, dunes famously not being designed for a speedy getaway.

Being back in her own body also was not helping. Why she

had changed back was beyond her but it was inconvenient in words that Mummy would not let her say. Inconvenient. Frustrating. Frightening.

"Would you stop running?"

The cockney voice took Sophie by surprise just long enough for her to stumble and faceplant into the sand that was stinging in its coldness.

"If you're going to cross a desert you have to treat it as a marathon, not a sprint," he called up, she'd forgotten that Brutus was nestled in her pocket, "slow and steady pace. Hey, you've got younger. Why'd that happen?"

"I don't know," Sophie sat up and wiped a sandy tear from her cheek, "I don't know anything."

"Hey, don't cry," the acorn looked at her with an awkward smile, "seriously, I don't know what to do about that."

"I want to go home," she sniffed, "I'm not supposed to be here."

"Wherever you are, that is where you should be, after all… no matter where you go, there you are," Brutus tried his best to be supportive, "and whatever is in front of you do it with the confidence that you'll get there."

"It's all well and good you saying do it with confidence," Sophie looked down into her pocket, "but I don't know what I'm doing, I don't know how to save the Kingdom. I've muddled my way through everything."

"So muddle with confidence," Brutus brushed off her rising temper, "I'll tell you a secret, nobody knows what they are doing. Every adult that you see every day is just muddling through as best they can, sometimes it works and sometimes it doesn't, but believing in yourself does make it easier."

Sophie was going to snap back but she found that she had

no words. Instead she quietly pulled her cloak tighter and got back to her feet.

"It's getting cold," Brutus said after maybe five more minutes of silent walking, "maybe you should take shelter in that cave in those rocks and wrap up warmer."

"I hadn't even noticed those," Sophie stared at the huge mound of orange slabs rising at an angle out of the sand.

The stars almost seemed to twinkle more brightly overhead as she made her way carefully down the dune toward the formation.

It was an unusual landmark, a slab of yellow orange stone rising at an angle into the sky from a sea of sand with other slabs arranged at angles around it. It looked like the kind of place a giant lizard-man might be hanging around waiting to pick a fight.

The sand lay smooth and undisturbed all around the rocks and it crunched slightly under the forming frost, a good sign at least that there probably weren't any beasties hiding in the dark waiting to jump out and go 'A boogie woogie woo'.

It was an awkward climb, not difficult but she did have to steady herself with her hands and she noticed that the stone was cold to the touch, whatever desert heat had been held within them had been sucked out by the Long Night.

The cave wasn't far up the rock face and as she got closer Sophie could see that the cave walls were smooth hewn as if they had been carved. The staircase not far to her left that she was going to pretend that she didn't see had definitely been carved. Maybe this place was some kind of landmark for when the Vam'Pyres had crossed the desert long ago from Trancelvania.

There was a faint blue glow coming from within the

artificial tunnel and she wondered if someone else was taking shelter here.

"Let me go first," Brutus jumped out of Sophie's pocket, "the Shadow People exiles could be using this as a base on their way to the Kingdom."

"I hadn't thought about that," Sophie came to the realisation that she was armed literally with only wishful thinking.

A faint trickling of water and the sound of a harp being plucked echoed up from the interior, just loud enough to drown out the noise of anything else that might be quietly watching from the shadows of the nooks and crannies.

Cautiously Sophie made her way through the gently sloping tunnel toward the blue glow, being careful to stick to one side and keep herself in shadow where possible.

Being lighter in step Brutus had opted to raise his fists and charge on ahead in whatever was the seed equivalent of berserker rage. Something down there was going to get its backside kicked, even if it meant shadow boxing.

"Well sod that then," his voice echoed back up the tunnel moments later, "nothing here but a stupid glowing pool."

A glowing pool? Sophie thought back to the mana well in the Tower of the Grand Magus, it was supposed to be blue when it was healthy.

She ran down the last of the tunnel and into a cavern that was little larger than her bedroom. In the middle of the cave was a small pool no bigger than her bed and into which a small but steady trickle of water fell from somewhere high in the ceiling to follow a path carved naturally into the rocks before dribbling into the pool.

And the pool didn't look like the bubbling well of distilled magic that she had seen in the tower, it just looked like water. Although it did somehow seem to be the source of the harp music.

Stretching her finger out toward the calm surface that rippled only where the small but steady stream of water fell she tried to forget the image of the wandering spirit of the Magus blasted from his body.

Her finger broke the surface and she felt only slightly cold and wet. It was only water.

The glow seemed to be coming from somewhere beneath the surface and the more she looked the deeper the pool seemed to become and the clearer the music seemed to get. But it did nothing else.

Sitting on a convenient rock next to the pool Sophie unstrapped her clunky walking boots and tipped a bootful of sand out of each. Then instead of putting them back on she stared down into the pool at a reflection that she was familiar with from her mirror every morning.

Eight year old Sophie Weaver. Trapped in a world being overtaken by nightmares and the last great hope to save the Kingdom, somehow. And she had to do it before an army of Vam'Pyres invaded or the world ended.

She had no doubt that the Shadow People had well-meaning intentions but an army turning up out of nowhere and saying 'It's for your own good' never seemed to work out much back home.

It was too much for an eight year old all by herself. She wished that she had Floppsy Bunny, he was the ideas man… rabbit.

Then she began to cry.

"Hey," Brutus placed a hand on her toe, "don't cry, I'll kick the snot out of anyone who comes near you."

"You're just an acorn," Sophie snapped, "just like Daisy is

a cow, Wikki is a heavy book, and Walker is nothing more than an oversize toy. I'm all by myself."

Brutus took a step away from her, the names meant little to him as he had only heard Walker mentioned once before, and he tried not to take it personally as she was clearly upset. But still, words can hurt.

"You aren't big on seeing the potential in people," he said as he turned his back to go off and sulk in the corner, "just an acorn. As for your friends, you haven't come this far by yourself, you may have gotten lost but you have not been abandoned."

Sophie watched as he kicked up a tiny cloud of dust before sitting on a pebble.

"Old muggins here, just an acorn, he's still hanging around for you," he jerked a thumb at his green shell, "and I'm sure your friends haven't given up, even if you have."

"No," a tiny, high pitched voice said and Sophie's eyes snapped to a lavender haired pixie clothed in purple and yellow who was sitting on the edge of the pool, "your friends have not given up on you."

*

Wikki was tossed into an empty cell in the hot depths under the tower and the body of Walker was thrown on top of him without a second thought. It took him more than a few moments to get out from under the seized limbs of the clockwork man.

Only then was he able to take in his surroundings, and it didn't instill him with hope.

The dungeon was definitely one built for function over form. It was one huge room lit by burning torches and with all manner of evil looking devices hanging from the walls. The floors and walls were grey stone damp with humidity and there were a dozen or more cells throughout the room all with four walls of black iron bars.

And the cells were all filled with people. None of the weird and wonderful creatures of Trancelvania, all humans. Men, women, and children. Farmers, adventurers, cooks, cleaners, warriors, school children, doctors, barbers, maidens and squires. The full spectrum of humanity held prisoner by these nightmares, and Wikki's pages briefly fluttered to pages referencing war crimes.

He could not count how many were held in the other cells but they were crammed tight and the people within all looked across at him in fear and hopelessness.

Why take all these prisoners? What could the nightmares possibly want with so many people? From their eyes Wikki had a feeling that they already knew, and they were terrified.

He felt a chill travel down his spine and flutter his pages.

Not wanting to think of such things he turned back to his fallen friend and flicked himself to a page entitled 'Automotive Repair'.

Walker lay with his face planted on the ground and his butt in the air, his key shaped cloak was flopped over his head and his spring-loaded limbs were seized with his knees bent.

Prising and wrestling Wikki was eventually able to get himself into position under the Clankydoodle, however it turned out Walker was far heavier than he looked.

With a heave and a huff and a puff the Tome managed to get the clockwork man to rock slightly but that was about it, he remained firmly planted face down butt up.

"Hmm," Wikki thought for a second before trying to wedge himself under Walker's shoulder for more leverage.

His little feet spun on the ground as he tried to gain traction but he still couldn't lift the weight.

"Why couldn't you have had an access panel in your bum? Come on, Wikki, think. With a long enough lever and a fulcrum a man could move the world."

Climbing back out from under the clockwork man he stamped his feet over to the side of the cell to examine the situation. Then seeing no other option he ran full pelt at Walker and threw himself into the side of his butt toppling the clockwork man over with a crash and a cloud of dust.

Standing to brush down his cover Wikki admired his work, Walker lying on his back with his feet locked in the air.

"If all else fails, brute force and ignorance," he said as he kneeled beside his friend, and then opened his chest, "oh dear."

Propping open the hood with the little metal support bar Wikki surveyed the remains, for that really was the most appropriate word, in the strictest sense Walker could no longer be called a clockwork man. His insides were more like what was left when a racecar comes to a sudden stop thanks to concrete.

The primary spring that constantly winded and was Walker's main source of power had snapped, and all that stored energy had caused the spring to explode through the mechanics in his chest.

Experimentally clicking a jammed gear in the intestine area caused the seized legs to go loose and fall limply to the ground.

"Oh Walker," Wikki put his hands on the open chest and closed his eyes to shut out the mangled gears, there was nothing in the world he could do for his friend.

*

Sophie didn't say anything as she stared at the little woman with gossamer wings who sat on the edge of the pool, adjusting her purple and yellow dress and giving the kind of broad smile normally reserved for sharks and Julia Roberts.

Pixies were a concept that she was on comfortable terms with, being an eight year old and familiar with pop culture, but seeing one in real life however took a moment of adjustment.

"I should introduce myself," the pixie brushed her long lavender hair back behind pointed ears, "I am Maicherry of the Fae, you can call me Cherry, Miss Weaver."

"I'm Sophie, and he's Brutus," she pointed over to the acorn who was pretending to huff in the corner with his back to them.

"Lovely to finally meet you," with her hand Cherry hinted that Sophie should wipe the tears from her cheeks, "I've been keeping watch over you since chapter one."

"Chapter?"

"Since you arrived in the cave of fireflies, you didn't see me," the pixie knotted her fingers together and leaned her chin on them, still radiating her smile, "and now you're here. I haven't had a Weaver visit my pool in years."

"That's a lot to unpack," Sophie looked around, looking for the simplest question first, "is this where you live… in a cave?"

"In a cave in the desert," Cherry gave a laugh, "bless me, no. Fairy pools are like portals to the Fairy Kingdom, or anywhere else if you know how to use them. I chose to be the guardian of this pool to help the Vam'Pyre exiles if they ever wanted to come home, and to keep them from using it for their own ends of course."

"Why help them at all, aren't they evil?"

"Everyone deserves a chance at redemption, some people just need guidance," she tilted her head at Sophie, "much like yourself, in a certain respect. You wouldn't take a wee step back would you?"

The little pixie fluttered into the air and drifted delicately to the ground like a falling leaf as Sophie did as she was asked and stepped away.

All of a sudden there was a flash of purple light and yellow sparkles that filled the room with a strange warmth and the plink-plonk of harp music got slightly louder.

A mist that smelled strangely of violets swirled around and there stood in place of the diminutive pixie a tall and slender woman, with long lavender hair that flowed down over her shoulders to pale skin and an elegant purple and yellow dress that stopped just above her knees.

And Brutus' jaw stopped only because it had hit the floor.

She was barefoot and her wings had formed into a delicate shawl like lace over her shoulders and going down her back.

"That's better," Cherry's voice had grown up along with the rest of her body, "being small is handy for getting in and out of tight spaces, but it can be so awkward and restrictive, don't you think?"

"It was a recent lesson for me," Sophie was in awe of the beautiful woman who stood before her, "I didn't know that pixies could do that."

"It takes a very long time to learn how to grow up," Cherry sat back by the pool, "but now much like yourself I can be any size that I choose."

"I don't think I have much choice in the matter," Sophie looked at her tiny hands, "I don't have any real control over anything."

"Oh nonsense," the fairy gave a dismissive wave, "you saw yourself as a princess, didn't you? You had a clear image of a beautiful green gown and flowing hair like your mother, didn't you?"

"Yes, but *ow-*"

Sophie stumbled forward as heels appeared under her feet but was caught by Cherry, who for some reason no longer seemed so tall.

"I was there when you arrived," the fairy smiled another wide smile, "remember?"

"Hey, you're you again," Brutus said with surprise, then remembering to keep up the pretense of the huff he turned his back on Sophie, but only just enough that he could still keep an eye on them.

"What?"

Her arms were long and slender once more and she was back in the flowing gown that she filled out so nicely, and then she thought about her feet and the heels turned to a pair of black leather boots more associated with the army and punk rock.

"How did you do this?"

"You did this, Sophie," Cherry smiled, "you're a princess of dreams, a Weaver."

"I don't understand," Sophie looked at her hands and then to Brutus, then to Cherry, and lastly to her reflection in the pool hoping an answer might be forthcoming from at least one of them.

"If you were asleep but knew that you were dreaming then you could change the dream around you, couldn't you, after all it is *your* dream?"

"I suppose..?"

"Ta-dah," Cherry placed her hands on Sophie's shoulders and held her tight, "this is a dream larger than you can imagine, a dream of the whole universe. That is your power, Weavers can change the dream, weave the dream around them."

"But how?"

"Confidence," Brutus called from his corner, trying to decide if he should keep up his passive-aggressive sulk, being huffy wasn't exactly impressive to the ladies.

"Yes, confidence," Cherry stroked a lock of Sophie's hair, "and strength, courage, wisdom, love, and compassion, but mostly you just have to see things as they ought to be."

A dream? Change a dream to change the world?

"One step at a time," Cherry said to answer the unasked question before slipping to one side along the pool, running a hand across the glowing but crucially still completely ordinary and mundane water, "it can show your friends if you want it to."

Looking at the mostly calm surface of the water shining blue from deep below the surface Sophie listened to the harp music streaming through that light from the Fairy Kingdom playlist.

"I want it to."

"Don't tell me," the fairy turned her eyes to the pool, "tell it."

"Show me my friends."

"With your mind," she placed a hand softly on Sophie's shoulder and gave a squeeze of encouragement, "and not with words, words are for communication, change comes from belief."

Staring at the pool the water remained crystal clear with the same blue glow from the depths. For just a moment there was the tiniest ripple before the surface became calm again.

Sophie concentrated harder and this time the surface whirl and then a jet of water squirted her in the face.

Suppressing a quiet laugh Cherry told her to try again; calmer, visualize, be confident. Don't scrunch up your face into funny expressions or ball your fists.

The surface of the water hissed with a burst of TV static before changing to an image of Walker lying on a stony floor with his chest open and Wikki looking at the mess of gears in despair.

"Oh, Walker," she stepped back in shock as she watched Wikki trying to repair him, she turned to Cherry, "he was supposed to be my guardian. I blamed him for not being there."

"Sometimes things separate people," Cherry stepped next to Sophie and looked down at the pool to survey the damage, "and not all things but some you can fix."

"How? I will, ok," she straightened, "how do I get there?"

"That's up to you," Cherry shrugged, "but you can fix your guardian from here."

"I can?"

"Weave him fixed," the fairy said, "you don't have to know the mechanics to fix it, just see him working again and trust in the process."

Sophie looked at the fairy and then back at the pool, at Walker. Wikki was poking here and there trying to figure out where to even begin, and was getting nowhere with the mass of broken parts.

Suddenly before him everything in Walker's chest began to glow golden until the light became so bright that Wikki could no longer look at it.

"Buttercup," Walker sat bolt upright.

"What did he say?" Sophie looked at Cherry.

"Walker," Wikki threw his arms around the clockwork man.

"He said buttercup," Brutus came to join the ladies by the pool with more than a little cockish swagger in his step having forgotten entirely why he was pretending to huff in the first place.

"What did you mean by buttercup?" Wikki asked, still not having let go.

"Sophie," Walker gently removed himself from the embrace, "do you not think with the green tunic and blonde hair that she looks a bit like a walking buttercup?"

"He's alive," Sophie's eyes beamed to Cherry, "I did it."

"You did," Cherry smiled, "the power to fix all of this is within you. Even nightmares are but dreams."

The image in the pool changed to a black tower in the middle of a fortress more horrible than even the worst school lunches, it was a vile place that looked to have melted into the earth.

"The Castle of Pandemonium," Cherry said as Sophie took a step back in revulsion, "formerly the city of Adastra. Nightmares are still only dreams, Sophie, remember that. You control them, they don't control you."

She looked at the tower but somehow it didn't frighten her, it was only just a dream. Of sorts. It did however give her a strong sense of revulsion, it reminded her of the feeling of being sick.

Looking at Cherry she was about to ask her to help but then she realised what it was that she had to do.

"Brutus," Sophie kneeled by the acorn, "I'm sorry for saying that you're just an acorn. You have a strength in you that-"

Brutus cut her off with a smile and a jump. He wasn't huffing with her, not really, he was waiting for her to get the confidence that she needed to do what she had to do.

"You don't have to ask me twice," he flexed and gave a wink to Cherry, "sounds like it will be a good fight."

"Great," Sophie turned to the fairy, "so, Castle of Pandemonium. What's our fastest route?"

"Through the pool," Cherry nodded, "they go anywhere and everywhere, that's why we guard them."

BEEF TENDERIZER

Daisy had been left with the Shadow Person, the one that had been called a Purse Loyal by the dark book that looked like all fifty shades of nastiness.

Walker had been thrown over the shoulder and carried off by some hulking brute in the kind of dull armour that was actually designed to be used in combat rather than for standing around looking fancy. That being said it could barely contain the mass of bulging muscle within, to the point that its use was still largely decorative, and the faceless helmet didn't appear to have any eyeholes although this didn't seem to be much of a hindrance.

Two other brutes of equal dimensions and dress ordered Wikki to follow with his mouth shut, and they marched after him with the same singlemindedness of a golum.

The Purse Loyal tugged on her makeshift harness and led her across the dry and lifeless courtyard toward an archway in the black stone walls that opened into yet another huge courtyard. The nightmares seemingly were big into open plan design.

The scruffy haired crook wiped a tear from his eye and Daisy noticed that his cocky swagger was now gone. Billy Brand had always worked on not meeting his employers no matter the job, if nothing else that made it easier to get away if he decide to keep the loot. Now he had broken that rule and he realised that he was involved in something far larger and far more sinister than simply catching some girl.

And he doubted that the Grimoire was going to let him go with his soul. Or payment.

Stopping to look up at the stars twinkling furiously overhead, for that was indeed what they were doing and he got the distinct impression that the fury was directed specifically at him, and the thought dawned that he wasn't just involved in something more sinister but also quite literally darker.

Looking back at Daisy and her big innocent face he couldn't help but feel guilty. He didn't want to find something to feed her to, she was just a stupid cow, what had she done to deserve that?

"Moo?"

"Come on," he slumped his shoulders and trudged them through the archway.

In the courtyard beyond were dozens of the same hulking brutes that had led away Wikki. Each one was identical in size and dimension to the others and all were wearing the same dark grey armoured breastplate and faceless pointed helmet with no eyeholes. There was more bulging muscle on display than backstage at a photo shoot for men's underwear.

The nightmare things seemed to suck all life out of the world around them, a fact that made Daisy wonder where they had managed to find so many Olympic power-lifters to form an army.

One of the brutes detached from the others and approached the Purse Loyal in the same slow but unstoppable momentum of a glacier, barring any further access to the courtyard, which suited the crook just fine.

"The cow is to be taken to the stables," Billy Brand said weakly, not able to look up at the blank faceplate staring down at him.

The brute held out a leather-gloved hand without a word and waited for Billy Brand to turn over the rein.

Hesitating for a moment he looked to Daisy and then at the outstretched slab of meat in a leather glove before him. It was the kind of hand that crushed boulders and dreams in the same way normal people squeezed stress balls. He handed over the leash and walked away as quickly as possible without looking like he'd lost his cool, which had at best already been hanging on by a ragged thread.

Daisy looked up at the faceless hulk before her and was nearly yanked off her feet as the brute suddenly set on a march toward a black outbuilding with black doors.

What was it with these guys and all the black anyway, were they not hugged enough when they were young and then got really into Norwegian Black Metal?

The brute said little more than a few animalistic grunts as he half led, half yanked Daisy toward the stable. It wasn't that she was dragging her feet; the brute marched to the beat of his own drum and each time she fell behind she was yanked forward like a shivering chihuahua by his relentless stride.

Opening the door led to a dark and musty corridor that clearly had not been used in some time. What straw there was that lay on the floor looked as though it was the original packing material for the Ark of the Covenant.

For some reason the brute led her to the last stable on the left despite almost every other unit lying empty. Perhaps they just intended to lock her up and forget about her, death by negligence?

As soon as he led her into the stable Daisy spun and did a one cow stampede that splattered him against the wall. Amazingly the brute was only stunned and began to get unsteadily to his feet.

Thinking fast Daisy jumped into the air and spun out a kick that would be pretty impressive being delivered from Jackie Chan let alone from someone whose socio-economic identity was 'dairy herd'. Her hoof collided with the huge head and sent the hulk into a tumble across the stables and made the heavy helmet tumble from his head.

'Do you know kung fu?' Daisy tried to say as she stood over her fallen opponent but it came out as "Moo?"

It was then that she noticed that the form was significantly smaller than before, and when she nudged the armour she found that it was almost hollow.

Rolling the chest-plate so he lay on his back Daisy saw a guy who badly needed a few hearty meals and a workout. The muscle-bound brute had somehow been replaced by a skinny farmhand in rags, and right before her eyes the armour began to crumble into ash.

All except for the helmet. Daisy narrowed her eyes and made a mental note of that fact.

Doing her best impression of tiptoeing she edged toward the entrance of the stables and peered out across the growing ranks of the hulk army.

There were significantly more steroid enthusiasts than she

could dropkick her way through without some kind of cinematic slow-motion effect or montage music.

Exploring the stables she found that the first few were filled with empty cardboard boxes in a surprising example of a separation at source approach to recycling.

Nuzzling her way through the cardboard she eventually came across a huge box for something called a Pony Entertainment System (a distinct and legitimate product do not steal). Flipping the box over herself she found that she could use the handle holes to see out through.

Cautiously she crept out the door being sure to keep an eye on the assembled ranks of the hulk army thankfully and suspiciously conveniently with their backs to her, and for any who might be on patrol.

The army seemed to be facing toward the tower listening to someone soapboxing or giving their 'and thus we go to war' speech and she was able to creep along with relative ease. Coming to the back row of muscle-bound troopers she hunkered down so it looked like the box had been abandoned and she tried to hear just what was being said to the brutes.

Whoever was speaking was too far away and she could not make out the actual words, just a tone that implied that violence was soon to ensue. Checking around her Daisy stood up and crept along the back of the rank, she would have to get closer to hear what was going on. And then she'd have to find the others.

'Ooh' she thought as she hunkered down quickly as a brute patrolled to the end of the rank, he looked around but ignored the box and started back on the same way that he had come.

Daisy stood again and crept further along the assembly of

brute troopers, taking care not to draw attention to herself. Coming to the end of the line she saw a well-trodden path that had been worn into the ground by the patrolling guard. But more than that she saw a hole in the wall with a stairwell leading down into it, and from which a group of men in shackles were being led up.

She made an educated guess that the stairwell was probably the path to the dungeons, but before she could gather her thoughts there was a curious 'huh?' from behind her.

The patrolling brute had spotted the box and was making his way toward her like an incoming glacier.

Waiting until the last second Daisy stood up and dragged the brute into the box and knocked the helmet from his head with a headbutt that really, really hurt.

The brute almost immediately transformed into a guy with a whip and three-day stubble, he looked a bit like a put-upon archeology professor.

If she had any further doubts about the evil in the helmets they were removed when she looked out the eyeholes again.

A brute was walking along the line of shackled men violently placing a helmet on each and with a pop of the universe making room each prisoner ballooned and their rags were replaced with rippling muscle and tarnished armour. With each brute there also came a metallic ping as the bonds of their shackles broke under the strain of the sudden growth spurt.

Daisy watched as they built a slave army of mindless brutes from the captured people, and she could make out one distinct word being repeated over and over with pure venom: Weaver.

The nightmares were creating an army just to hunt Sophie. Suddenly Daisy was in full view of all and turning around she found herself staring up at the blank faceplate of one of the brutes.

And in that moment she felt the primordial rage of herbivores everywhere when a predator threatens the herd. She narrowed her eyes…

****

The following scene has been censored due to its extreme graphic violence.
Please enjoy these doodles by the author instead
****

*

"Buttercup!"

Walker sat bolt upright and Wikki jumped backward in shock, and then he threw his arms around the mechanical man.

"Walker," it was quite an awkward hug as the clockwork man's chest was still propped open, "What did you mean by buttercup?"

"Sophie," he casually but firmly pulled himself out of Wikki's enthusiastic embrace, "do you not think with the green tunic and blonde hair that she has the appearance of a walking buttercup?"

"Can't say that I've thought about it."

Looking down into his exposed innards he saw cogs of gold tick-tocking along yet geared in a way that he had never seen before, but it seemed to be a heck of a lot more efficient.

"What did you do?"

"It wasn't me," Wikki said as Walker closed up his chest with a click, "first you started glowing, then you were fixed. There wasn't an in between step."

"Is Sophie here?"

Having sprung to his feet Walker then climbed up the bars of the cells to look over the heads of the other prisoners. The cages of the room seemed to be filled with the population of a fairly substantial town, all looking a bit undernourished and worse for the wear. But no blondes big or small.

"No Sophie," Wikki said, "but it looks like they didn't know what to do with the people who lived here after they took over."

A heavy creak like a cat made of rust dragging claws made

of rust down a rusty chalkboard screeched through the dungeon as a lock turned and then the heavy wooden door at the end of the room drifted open on surprisingly well maintained hinges.

Standing in the doorway was a lot of muscle thinly disguised as a man that was barely contained within a steel breastplate and pointed helmet with the face obscured by a blank faceplate. The brute stamped so heavily across the dungeon floor that Walker felt his gears shake.

Stopping at a cell full of shackled men he opened the door and grasped their chain with little more than a grunt, leading them outside with a yank that pulled the first three men from their feet.

"I assume they have figured out what to do with the population," Walker watched the brute lead the men into the night outside and then another brute slammed the dungeon door with a boom like a blast from God's shotgun.

Some of the people in the other cells began to cry and others looked across at Walker and Wikki in a way that implied 'the bad guys usually keep the heroes separate for dramatic effect so isn't it about time you did something heroic?'

At that moment a crackle of electricity sparked in the room as a ball of lightning appeared in the cell above the heroes and its edges began to swirl as it formed into a swirling vortex.

"This is not good, we are in a metal cage and I am made of metal," Walker crouched back, "not a good combination."

"I don't know what you're worried about," Wikki crouched back into another corner, "you aren't the one who is flammable."

A clarity like glass began to appear in the centre of the vortex and grew until it formed a circular window that was only fringed by the electricity, and it seemed to be looking at a rocky ceiling.

All of a sudden a ball of green and gold fell through with a slightly surprised, "Ooh."

Pulling the hem of her dress down from over her head Sophie looked up at the others.

"Hi guys," she said, standing just in time for an acorn to bounce off her head. She looked up at the fairy pool in time to see Cherry give her a thumbs-up before the vortex softly drifted apart like mist.

"Sophie," Walker and Wikki rushed over and said in remarkable synchronicity, "you should not be here."

"I'm pretty sure this is exactly where I have to be," she looked around the cold, grey dungeon, "before an army of Vam'Pyres invades Trancelvania and everything goes to buggery."

That pretty much summed up everything that she had seen since falling from the airship, but for completeness sake Sophie gave a rundown from the dead city to meeting Brutus, and the truth about the Shadow People and how they were sending an army to fight the nightmares.

The general consensus was that they had to do something fast before everything went to, as previously mentioned, buggery.

"We've met the nightmares," Wikki looked at Walker's chest, "I've never seen anything like them before. And they had a demonic book, a Grimoire working for them."

"They do not look like they have a physical form," Walker added, "they were like spectres or something, half ghost and half something else. I do not know if we can hurt them."

"The first thing we have to do is get out of this cell," Sophie said, cracking her knuckles and staring at the big lock built into the door, a grinding and crunching sound coming from within as she scrunched up her nose in concentration.

"I think you are supposed to imagine it being open and it will be," Brutus had a bit of a crush on Cherry and had been paying a lot of attention to her voice, "I think you'd actually have to know the mechanics of picking a lock to do what you're trying to do."

The lock glowed gold and exploded in a brief flash of sparks and gears.

"Whoops," she flushed briefly red, "well, it's open now."

"Or that works too."

"Sophie," Walker placed a hand on her shoulder, "promise me the next time you try to fix me that you will just use a screwdriver."

As she stepped into the dungeon proper she looked at the rows upon rows of menacing torture devices, most of which she didn't even want to imagine how they worked, and one or two that looked like they defied the laws of physics.

And then she turned to look at the other cells; there must have been ten or more and all filled with frightened people who now looked at her with a glimmer of hope.

She imagined the people getting out and one by one the doors around the dungeon popped open in a Mexican wave of emancipation. Timidly the prisoners stepped out, they were still in the dungeon in the middle of a doom fortress so freedom was a bit of a lose term.

"They were separating the men," Wikki said as the crowd

of mostly women and children began to approach the group, "I don't know where they were taking them."

"Sophie," Walker looked around the prisoners, they weren't exactly in the condition to man the barricades and storm the Bastille, "can you get them out of here?"

Probably, but where could she send them that they would be safe? And how-

"Cherry," Brutus jumped, "she can take them to the Vam'Pyres."

"Send them to an invading army?" Walker's eyebrow raised with an audible whirl, "That is a novel suggestion."

"They're only invading because they didn't know if I could stop the nightmares," Sophie lit up, "if I send the freed prisoners to them for protection they'll know that I'm doing something. It might even cause them to stop the invasion."

"Or you could be sending them from one prison to another."

"I've been in what they call a prison," Sophie started to think about Cherry's pool, "believe me they will be better off."

A ball of lightning appeared before Sophie and it began to swirl until a wall of rock appeared within, and then Cherry's head appeared from an odd angle with a curious look on her face.

"Cherry, can you get these people out of here," Sophie looked back at the prisoners, "and take them to the Shadow People army?"

"Easy done," she said, "they've camped about one dune over. Send the people through, but tell them to take a running jump or they'll fall back into the pool."

"Ok, you heard the lady," Walker started ushering the

crowd, "a running jump, the Weaver is getting you out of here."

That single name spread through the crowd like wildfire and fear was replaced with hope. One by one the crowd started forward forming a more or less orderly line as they moved toward the swirling vortex of the fairy pool.

"Come on," Cherry coaxed them on, extending her gossamer wings to show them that it wasn't some trick.

One after the other they ran and jumped through the vortex and fell out of sight as they popped through and gravitational 'up' was suddenly in a different direction.

"What about the men?" A woman with a little boy stopped with Sophie, "Will they be ok?"

"We'll get them out," Sophie rubbed the boy's cheek in a way that her Nanna would, even though in reality she was probably about the same age as the boy and he'd be pushing her over in the schoolyard because girls have cooties, "we'll bring them back with the sun."

"Queen Sola," the woman said, "it is said our Queen was born of the sun; she started going mad when the moon disappeared, that was the same time those nightmares first fell upon us."

Sophie thought back to what she had seen in the Tower of the Grand Magus, the void that had appeared over some unknown tower, and the Queen who talked with him.

The Queen was linked to the sun, and the nightmares had destroyed the Grand Magus and an entire city to grow their power and turn the world to darkness.

A tremendous smashing and crashing came from beyond the door that led out of the dungeon. It sounded like there was a war going on and the gang looked at one another, had some scout force from the Vam'Pyres got here and it had all kicked off?

"I'll find the men," Sophie rushed the woman along with the crowd to the vortex, "and your Queen."

Something heavy crashed against the door and then it banged again, and again but harder. Puffs of dust shot from between the wooden slats of the door as they strained against another heavy blow.

"Do you think they know that we're getting everybody out of here?" Walker strode around the vortex and drew his cutlass adopting a fencing stance aimed at the door.

"Probably," Wikki raised his fists in the closest thing he could to a fighting pose (p117 of Hieronymus Punch's *The Revised Rules of Pugilism for the Country Gent*), "the Grimoire probably has a seeing glass."

"I'll handle this, chums," Brutus stepped in front of the others and held his arms like he was carrying a large box under each.

The door exploded open as one of the hulking brutes bounced across the dungeon floor and slammed against the bars of the nearest cell, out for the count.

There must have been a fire outside as the room was flooded with a hot orange light and the smell of smoke, and then an angry black shadow stepped into the doorway.

The silhouette was hunkered forward ready to attack and the trio took a step in unison back toward Sophie.

And then the shadow stepped forward.

"Daisy!"

THE BAND BACK TOGETHER

Daisy nuzzled Sophie and Walker delighted to see them both alive and well, especially surprising considering that the last time she had seen Walker he was lying in a pool of his own coolant.

Somehow a red strip of cloth had become wrapped around her head like a bandana and she ducked out of the way every time that Sophie tried to take it off, a movement that was awkward enough as Wikki was currently hugging her neck and hanging off her like an ill-fitting cowbell.

Some of the people who had been fleeing through Cherry's pool had stopped to watch the happenings but with a 'moo' of instruction they continued to run and jump through the portal and out of sight.

As the last of the prisoners fled and the portal once more faded out of existence Daisy walked the gang over to the brute that she had kicked through the door, lying unconscious and upside down against one of the now empty cells.

Looking down at the monstrous bulk of the fallen brute

Sophie wondered how he could see through that blank faceplate from under which there came gentle snoring sounds.

Using her hoof Daisy gently pushed the helmet up until it fell away to reveal a chubby face that was oddly out of place on the Olympic sized body, and within seconds the muscular frame became that of a fella who really needed to spend less time indoors.

"That is what happened to the men," Walker looked to Sophie with a sudden understanding, "they are making a slave army of mindless brutes."

"Moo," Daisy confirmed.

"Let's go," Sophie started toward the door and the glowing orange light beyond, "I know how to bring back the sun, we have to rescue the Queen."

"The Queen?" Walker started after her as Daisy trotted along with Wikki and Brutus mounted on her back.

"She is connected to the sun somehow," Sophie had a fierce look in her eye, "this all started when the moon darkened. I think you were right about the omen, I think the nightmares did it to seize the Queen."

Stepping through the door and up the short flight of stairs into the courtyard the gang was greeted with a scene of total devastation.

The whole courtyard was dotted with smoking craters and burning rubble. To one side was a massive pile of the faceless helmets of the brutes and on the other were several piles of unconscious men.

Everyone turned in slow motion to look at Daisy.

"Moo?"

"Stinky Sophie?"

A voice came from an archway to their right and the gang

saw Billy Brand standing with a dumb look of shock at the scene before him, then whatever wits he still possessed snapped a short journey back into place.

"Guards, guards!" He drew his long, thin blade as he called for backup, "the Weaver is here."

The ground began to shake and there came a sound like a gravel path being chewed, the sound of an awful lot of feet in combat boots marching as one.

A horde of the hulking brutes trooped into the courtyard to form up ranks behind the Purse Loyal.

"I think that we may have lost the element of surprise," Walker readied his cutlass as the enemy force advanced.

"Moo," Daisy shook her head so the ends of her bandana were flicked back behind her ears.

Suddenly a three foot spider popped into existence between the group and the advancing army, which itself had stopped moving as Billy Brand froze in terror.

And then another one appeared, and another one, and on and on until a small army of arachnids now stood between the two sides.

"Miss Weaver?"

"Hi, Archie," Sophie waved, "we found the ones who made the sun disappear but we could sort of do with a little help, what with them having a slave army and all."

The spiders looked around at the mob behind them; one boy so white that he would make a snowman look bronzed, and a whole bunch of human tree-trunks standing stupidly waiting for an instruction.

"They don't look like they do much," Archie said, "and I think that the boy may have soiled himself."

"That's because he was rude to you before and is probably hoping that you aren't holding a grudge," Sophie looked at the school bully, and then at the army behind him, "if you knock the helmets off the slaves they become normal people again."

When no orders were forthcoming from their alleged leader muscle memory took the initiative and there came a crunch of boots on stone as the brute force marched forward with axes raised. They may have lacked any agency of their own but the helmets came pre-programmed with a propensity for mindless violence.

Billy Brand took this as his cue to slowly start walking backward in one of Sun Tzu's lesser regarded strategies: the hasty retreat.

Something that the brutes were too dumb to consider due to all the magical equivalent of steroid abuse is that when spiders rear up on their back two pairs of legs they have twice the number of arms as a human. And spiders are fast.

The sound of rapid punching filled the air like a squad of boxers beating the ever-loving snot out of a meat packing plant. Axes, helmets, the occasional codpiece all flew through the air as the spiders made short work of the slave force.

"Go do what you need to do, Miss Weaver," Archie sent a helmet flying and then let the unconscious man drop, he turned his eyes and saw Billy Brand slinking along the wall, "I'll have a word with your friend here."

The conversation wasn't lost on the creeping Billy Brand and he broke into a screaming run with Archie scuttling after him.

"The entrance to the tower is on the other side of that wall," Wikki led them away from the fight toward the archway that they had passed through after having first met the nightmares.

Running to it they saw that it opened into another courtyard, this one deliberately wide and open to reveal the grandeur that would have been here if it weren't for all the corruption.

"Oh, nuts," Walker looked beyond the tall gates in the fortress wall to the town beyond and saw what could only be described as a sea of muscle and iron helmets looking off toward the outer walls, "they must have enslaved everyone in the county."

Like a tide the huge assembly of brutes turned in the direction of the gang. They were confused and looked around one another dumbly, they had been told that the 'bad guys' would be coming from outside of the fortress. Some scratched their helmets and wondered if they were supposed to fight whilst others hoped that somebody else would make the decision for them.

"Quick," Brutus ran forward, "close the main gates, I can hold them back!"

"Not by yourself," Walker looked at Sophie and then ran after him.

Reaching one of the heavy gates Brutus started pushing but it didn't budge until Walker and Sophie arrived to help. Daisy and Wikki braced themselves against the other gate and pushed with all their might.

It slowly dawned on the slave army that they were about to be locked out of the fortress and they had better do something about that. They began to march and as the gates got closer together their march turned into a charge.

As the gates closed Sophie and Walker struggled with the heavy lock but with a kick on the gates from Daisy they managed to drop the heavy bar in place just as the brute army hit it. The wood groaned as thunderous blows landed against the gates and they actually moved enough that a cracking sound shot from the locking bar.

"Get up the tower," Brutus turned to Sophie holding back the brutal clashes with his little hands, "I can hold them here."

"There is such a thing as overconfidence."

"Sophie," he gave her a look of determination, "what am I?"

"My friend," another crack shot from the gate.

"Thanks," he smiled, "and what else?"

"An acorn?"

"Exactly," he turned to face the gate and slammed one foot on the ground so hard that it broke right through the paving stone, and then he slammed the other foot too through the frosty stone as well.

"It has been my honour to help a Weaver, and to be your friend," he looked back to give Sophie and the group one last smile, "you guys may want to take a step back."

Turning to the gate Brutus held out his hands and let a scream that sounded like a war cry. His shell split apart and his arms shot up and out as his legs burrowed into the ground and tore up the stone paving of the courtyard.

He pressed against the gate and broke through a keystone above growing bigger and wider and stronger.

"Wow," Walker said.

"Moo," agreed Daisy.

For a long time Sophie didn't say anything, she simply stared at the gate now solidly closed by an enormous and immovable oak tree, its leaves swaying gently under the twinkling stars.

"Thank you, Brutus," she whispered and then turned to

the stairs leading into the tower as the first few flakes of snow started to fall, "let's go."

*

The interior of the tower smelled old and stale as if everything that was once good had been left to wither and rot.

There was something squiffy going on with the architecture too. Doors that should have led to rooms opened out into balconies whilst the very door next to it could open into the dungeon. On more than one occasion Walker had went to check that they weren't being followed and the room behind had become somewhere else entirely.

"It's the logic of a nightmare," Wikki said, "being trapped in a maze that keeps changing."

"Nightmares are still just dreams," Sophie remembered Cherry's words and a sound came like the dull whomp of an underwater explosion and reality rippled around them in a pulse of unceremonious grey light.

"What in the stars was that?"

"I think I just fixed the logic," Sophie walked to the door ahead and opened it.

The room beyond was a throne room, and sitting on a twisted monstrosity that might once have been described as the seat of the Kingdom was the cracked black leather and chain wrapped Grimoire. He was somewhat surprised to see the prisoners, and the girl that he assumed must be the Weaver.

"You're trespassing, girl," the evil book quickly regained his air of contempt, "and didn't I order you other three to the afterweave?"

"Moo," Daisy snorted meaning a word that won't be translated for the benefit of our younger readers.

"Leave this one to me," Wikki marched ahead of the group, "this is a literary problem."

The Great Hall was behind the throne room and Sophie could sense the presence of the nightmares brooding within.

"You can handle this?" Walker asked as he and Daisy followed Sophie in an arc around the two books who were moving to square off.

Wikki simply nodded, he was not willing to take his eyes off the dark book that had slithered from the throne and moved toward him with a lolling gait like disease embodied.

"Don't go far, you three," the Grimoire gave a dismissive wave to the door on the other side of the throne room and a squad of slave brutes trotted in with axes raised, "it will save us the bother if you stay close."

Daisy turned to face the new enemies but not before looking to Walker and Sophie, she gave a nod to where the nightmares hid and then flicked back the strands of her red bandana.

As the first bright bolt of magic burst from the Grimoire's spiny fingertips Daisy was silhouetted delivering a vicious drop kick to the goolies of the nearest brute.

Walker tried to take the lead but at this point Sophie was powering ahead on the combination of determination and pure adrenaline of a child knowing that there was ice cream at the end of the homework. Reaching the big double doors she braced herself against the cold old wood and pushed both doors open wide.

Moving with a ponderous groan the doors revealed a musty old Great Hall with a long banquet table covered with dust and plates of long rotten food.

But the room was dominated by a huge old stone fireplace that stretched maybe twelve feet up the wall and was engraved with old runes and Celtic lines.

A bent figure wrapped in a tattered black shawl stood by the fireplace staring at the cold ash lying in the hearth.

"They came to take everything from me," the voice was frail and old, she never looked away from the ash, "and now you come to take what little remains."

"Your majesty," Sophie looked around the room, she knew the nightmares were here hiding in some dark corner, "I've come to bring back the sun. I don't want to take anything from you."

Whispers insinuated around the Hall, barely on the edge of hearing but insidious enough to fill the air.

"Liar."

"Falsehoods."

"She has come for you."

"She has come for your family."

"The end is near."

"She has come to take all."

"You will have nothing."

"Nothing."

"Alone."

Walker circled around with his cutlass drawn, "Where is that coming from?"

"The clockwork man."

"Not welcome."

"Should be dead."

"Wants to take all."

"Power is growing."

"Dangerous."

"Finish her now."

Queen Sola turned her eyes to Sophie, they were pale and utterly sightless but she could still sense the power of the Weaver.

"Your majesty," Sophie took a step forward, "I'm here to bring back the light and warmth of day."

"Liar!" the Queen threw up her hands and a burst of black origami birds shot toward Sophie who ducked with a surprised squeak and the birds burst into ash on the wall behind her.

At that same time the nightmares erupted from the high shadows and dove toward Walker. He slashed at the first creature to come close but the blade passed harmlessly through its misty body and as he twirled the blade it became tangled in the cloth of a tattered curtain.

Yanking at the cutlass he tore the curtain from the railing to reveal a balcony and a night sky with the stars twinkling furiously overhead as the incoming snow storm started to grew on the horizon.

Sophie ducked behind a chair as another blast of paper birds shot past her and broke into ash on the stone floor. She tried to imagine the Queen shining or for light in some form to creep back into her life.

"For over a year my family has been lost to me," the blind Queen hissed, "you will not take the last of me."

She let forth another painful burst of paper birds but Sophie rolled out of the way behind a credenza that had helpfully stepped out from the wall to provide cover.

Her family? She looked at the nightmares circling Walker framed against the window to the night sky as he slashed impotently at them.

The stars. They had been twinkling brighter and brighter since she got here. The sun was a star. The stars were her family.

She pushed a chair down in front of the Queen. The stars could not be seen during the day because the sun was shining so bright, and moonlight was reflected sunlight. That was how she could see her family, reflected in the moonlight, and the nightmares darkened the moon a year ago.

Grabbing the fallen curtain Sophie threw it over the Queen who screamed in rage as the Weaver ran to the balcony door.

One of the nightmares froze for just a moment watching Sophie and was about to whisper its poisoned voice when Walker's cutlass sliced through its porcelain doll face. The mask fell in two pieces and shattered on the cold floor causing the creature to drift apart in a whispered scream.

"Our brethren."

"Murderer."

"Weakness."

The three nightmares circled wider as Walker slashed out again and only narrowly missing another as Sophie threw open the balcony doors to a blast of icy wind.

"Weaver."

"Stop."

Throwing one hand into the air Sophie watched the darkness begin to pull back like a curtain across the face of the moon and light teased like a halo around its edges. It began to swirl into a pool like a black sea on the lunar surface until it reached out like an enormous teardrop.

The Queen threw off the curtain and levelled her hands to unleash another blast of black origami birds when a wisp of electric light popped into existence behind her. And from the wisp came a pixie who quickly became an enormous owl that pounced on the Queen's shoulders and pushed her to the ground behind Sophie.

"No."

"Stop."

"Do not do it."

The nightmares whispered as the horror they had created turned on themselves and in their confusion Walker was able to shatter a second mask, banishing the creature back to the void it had come from.

The Queen could see a growing halo of light and one by one a twinkle began to appear in her blackened vision, and suddenly the majesty of the whole night sky opened before her and she wept with joy.

The teardrop of darkness hanging from the moon burst and a stream of black energy shot across the night sky to the balcony and Sophie screamed as every drop of it wrapped her up in thick oil and filled her through her mouth, nose, ears, and pores.

*

Daisy back flipped three times across the throne room before diving feet first into the chest of a brute who was caught mid-swing of his huge axe.

A cinematically impressive fight sequence had broken out as she fought to keep the squad of brutes away from Wikki who was sitting in a magical bubble under an onslaught of dark and foul smelling magic.

Kicking the helmet off a felled brute to release the man from slavery she then rolled into another brute and bowled him over with her udders before knocking him out with a headbutt.

As that helmet too was knocked to the corner the room was lit as another burst of light came from the spindly fingertips of the Grimoire.

"Bound in darkness,
chains and decay;
with whips and straps
to maim and flay;
Blow this wretched Tome away."

Ancient and foul lettering lit up the room as a blast of fel magic crackled like lightning across the room and shattered against the magical shield surrounding Wikki. He was holding himself back, working on one big spell that he have to time perfectly as he would only get one shot.

"Bind in a mask of exquisite pain;
wrap in a darkness that will forever stain;
remove from this world
my walking bane,
Curse him with all this world's disdain."

The ghost of an angry skull like something you'd see airbrushed on the side of a van appeared over Wikki and smashed itself against the bubble of his shield and shattered out of existence. However it also caused the finest of hairline cracks to appear in the magical dome.

"Darkness binding strife
Pain and anger hold him tight
Jaws of death now bite."

A ghostly dragon wrapped itself around the bubble and snapped its maw shut around the shield causing the bubble to crack in its teeth and then it burst in a wave of magic. The Grimoire's sense of satisfaction was short lived as too late he realised that Wikki had already begun a spell, his one shot.

"Snap away reality, bye bye gravity, gone from the world today, you're smoked, so mad, give up, begone now, the world don't want you, the time has come for you, end this existence, pay your penance, get out, no escaping, your hold is breaking, time is quaking, lose yourself,"
Wikki held both hands up as the Grimoire tried desperately to rush through a spell, the Tome smiled as he sighted between his thumbs, *"unbind!"*

The Grimoire blew apart as all its binding burst at the seams; chains and leather straps flew across the throne room as the corrupted demonic pages burned to ash fluttering in the air.

One final brute helmet bounced across the floor as Wikki walked to the twisted leather cover that was slowly burning out of existence.

Looking down at the ashen remains of the evil book he understood exactly why they had been sent back to the demonic realm from whence they came, as much as he was against censorship these things were not meant for this world.

"You're out of print."

Daisy came to his side, her fur was damp with sweat and her bandana ragged at the edges but she was otherwise unharmed.

"That was page 8 of Mssr M. Mathers *Radical Adapted Prestidigitations*," Wikki said to her curious look.

With the destruction of the Grimoire the slave helmets

began to crumble to dust all around them as the corrupt magic became unbound, and the brutes all through the fortress were released from the twisted power.

And then they heard Sophie scream.

*

Walker ran to Sophie and caught her as she fell unconscious to the floor.

The nightmares meanwhile had moved to hover around the Queen to whisper hollow words and empty threats. They were held at bay by the giant owl standing guard that flapped its mighty wings and snapped at the masks of the creatures as they tried to come close.

But it was too late and the words were falling on deaf ears as Queen Sola knelt on the ground crying at the beauty of the moon and the stars.

"Brothers and sisters," she sobbed happily, "I see you."

In the twinkling language known only to the heavens the stars explained what had happened and what had been done to save her and the Kingdom.

Her clothes had changed from black to regal blues and her tired grey hair had turned to radiant blonde, she had become a young Queen again.

And then the stars told her about Sophie.

"Oh child," the Queen turned to see Walker cradling the unconscious little girl.

The door burst open as a cow and a Tome appeared, ready to fight, but they immediately dropped their guard upon seeing the Queen.

"Hey, the Oracowl," Wikki said as the nightmares slowly retreated toward the shadows.

The Oracowl began to glow and its wings turned to gossamer as it stood tall and proud, its legs growing long and fine, behind its eyes grew ears that were slender and pointed whilst its head feathers became flowing lavender hair. She was looking distinctly less avian and a lot more like a Fairy Queen.

"Your majesty," Maicherry of the Fae bowed her head in deference to the Queen before turning her eyes to Sophie.

"Your majesty," Queen Sola replied to the Queen of the Fairies.

"No, my majesty," Sophie said in a voice of a thousand screaming whispers as a wave of darkness rippled out from her body knocking everyone back as she rose into the air.

Walker stared in shock at the monster now floating in the centre of the room; long black hair that was slick with a foul grease, skin grey and cracked, teeth sharpened to fangs, eyes glowing green and seeping a fel mist.

"You have delivered onto me the perfect vessel," the Nightmare Queen's voice oozed into their ears, "in return I will visit upon your kingdoms the most exquisite of horrors as I remake each and every being in this land in my glory."

As she spoke dozens of porcelain masks popped into the air around her and misty bodies began to take form as she created countless new nightmares. The other nightmare creatures came to join their Queen as the nightmare now had taken control.

"No," Walker rushed out and grabbed Sophie, wrapping his arms around her, "I know you are in there, Sophie, wake up from this nightmare."

The nightmare creatures circled around and the Nightmare Queen did not so much as struggle in Walker's grasp, she knew that he would not harm her vessel.

"I can unmake you with a thought, Clankydoodle."

"You control the nightmares, Sophie, they do not control you," Cherry said as she helped Queen Sola to her feet, "they are still only dreams."

"Come on," Walker removed Floppsy Bunny from his satchel and held it tightly to the Nightmare Queen, "I miss that lost little buttercup."

Something twitched and the Nightmare Queen became agitated, she started to struggle in vain against the immovable robot grip. She tried to make the clockwork man vanish but something inside of her was fighting, the Weaver wouldn't let her hurt Walker.

Queen Sola put her arms around Walker and the struggling nightmare.

"It's alright," Sola stroked the oily black hair, "the nightmare is over. It's sunrise."

Blinding sunlight cut into the room and the dozens of nightmare masks evaporated in whispered screams and the room filled with light as dawn broke over Trancelvania.

The blackness vanished from the tower as beautiful blue tiled spires on white walls rose into the sky and the purple void over the tower was consumed in the brightness of the rising sun.

The gates were thrown open as darkness was driven out and Adastra became the shining capitol it had been before the Long Night, the river ran clear and blue, a new gate appeared as a garden grew around the mighty oak Brutus standing in the new Park of the Old Gate.

Waves of green fields spread across the Cracked Vale in the ripple of morning sunlight carrying the power of the Weaver, infusing life in the parched ground and the light bringing with it the promise of a new day.

The rising dawn burst the bubble of forgotten time around

Slumberg as the city was restored and the people went about their daily lives unaware of the fate now lost in a nightmare. In his ever watchful Tower of Tahl the Grand Magus smiled into the crystal blue of his mana well as he watched the sun rise over the city of Adastra and spread over Trancelvania.

The lily-like shelters gracefully opened over Paris'Häl to shade the people of the city from the beautiful light that would otherwise burn their pale skin. Watching the lilies open the Duchess Ayri'Elle gave thanks that the Weaver had come. The Vam'Pyre army in the desert covered themselves as they made shelter around Cherry's cave and fetched water for the freed prisoners.

Dawn broke over Cuddleton and Sophie's trees turned slowly once more into the wood of the Inn of the Counting Sheep. The farming folk went back to work as if the Long Night had never happened; they had more important things to do than worry about the goings-on in places with palaces and the like.

And in a beautiful banquet hall little Sophie Weaver found herself kneeling on the ground being hugged by her mother and her father and everything felt alright now.

"We're always here for you," her mother wiped a happy tear from her eye.

"Your lucining is done," her father smiled like Walker, "time to wake up, Buttercup."

..EPILOGUE

MORNING HAS BROKEN

In the early morning Sophie awoke bouncing and full of energy, much to her mother's surprise. She was so happy and couldn't wait to get to school and back to her friends, which in itself made her mother worry that it was some kind of fever induced manic episode.

Daddy did not stay last night again, but it was ok because he was going to pick her up from school and take Sophie to her grandmother's house for dinner, and maybe ice cream.

She spent the morning singing some silly lullaby about cows sailing over golden trees, which gave them a break from jumping over moons. It was a kind of freeform thing that she was making up as she went along and it occurred to her that maybe she should write it down. She loved singing and she loved writing, it would be fun to start writing her own songs, even if they made only slightly more sense than Yellow Submarine.

Going through the library of fairy tale and horsy books on her bookshelf she found the journal that Daddy had bought her but that she had never used, she drew a daisy on the cover and titled the book 'Wikki Songs'. And the title of her first song she decided would be 'Walker and the Queen of the Sun'.

As Mummy drove her to school she scribbled the lyrics in her Wikki as fast as they would come to her. It was a song about two people drifting apart but coming together when they were needed most. And there was a bit of swashbuckling too, because everyone loves a bit of adventure.

Sophie had no idea where the lyrics were coming from, but they did seem oddly familiar. Like a dream or something that teased on the edge of memory.

She stared out of the window as they drove past a field of brown Jersey cows and she found herself wondering what it would be like if cows could do kung-fu. She giggled at the thought of udders flying everywhere and they would probably squirt milk every time they hit a bad guy. She wondered if they could be used like a water gun to blind the baddies in a fight.

Coming into town they passed the construction workers putting up concrete blocks for some new big shopping centre on the edge of town. Daddy once complained that it would kill the businesses in the town centre, Sophie had no real opinion on the matter because she thought shopping was boring. She was more interested in it as it was now, a lot of grey concrete on a building site like a fortress falling into ruin backwards.

When they stopped outside school Sophie kissed Mummy on the cheek and dropped her Wikki into her schoolbag. Then she said goodbye to Floppsy Bunny in the seat next to her and hopped out of the car into the stream of kids flowing through the gate into the school grounds.

The old grey bell tower of the school loomed ahead of her, usually seeing it filled her with a certain dread about another long and boring day filled with sums and stuff but today she smiled and was excited to see her friends.

Stopping by the black gates something caught her eye and she kneeled down next to the gate.

"Hi there," she said, "do you mind coming with me for a minute?"

As she reached out she heard her name being called and saw her friend Cheryl waving over.

Sophie smiled and ran to her friends who told her how cool it was that she got to take three days off school. Vomiting and dizziness is after all a small price to pay for no homework.

Suddenly she was knocked forward as a ginger haired boy with a rat-face nudged her as he walked by.

"Watch where you're going, Stinky Sophie."

"Hey, Billy Brand," Sophie smiled and held out her hand, "do you want to meet my new friend?"

She opened her fingers and the colour drained from Billy Brand's already pale face as Sophie offered him the small but hairy spider that she had plucked from the gate.

"Get away," he quivered on the spot.

"It's only a little spider," she took a step forward, "I think he'd like to be your friend."

"Get away," other boys had turned to see as he backed away from little Sophie Weaver.

"Take him," she stepped closer again and Billy Brand ran away screaming as he swatted at the spiders he now imagined were in his hair and down the back of his shirt.

And Sophie's friends laughed at the bully getting his

comeuppance. The other boys laughed as well, but most of them hoped that she kept her distance as they weren't overly fussed on spiders either.

The bell rang for class and everyone started to filter into the building, time for the boring part between break times. *Usually the boring part* but after three days in bed it was a welcome change and she was now so full of ideas she couldn't wait to be at her desk.

Thanking the spider for his help Sophie let the little arachnid down onto a nearby wall and as she did she heard an owl hoot from somewhere in the grove of trees beyond the school grounds.

And in an old oak tree watching little Sophie Weaver skip merrily into school Cherry sat on a branch with a wide smile on her face, with a giggle at her own little secret, for there is more to this world that the grown-ups have forgot but that children still see.

If you were looking at her right now she might flash you a smile and say, "Ssh."

ROW ROW ROW YOUR BOAT,

GENTLY DOWN THE STREAM,

MERRILY MERRILY MERRILY MERRILY,

LIFE IS BUT A DREAM.

-JAMES T KIRK, CAPTAIN
SPEAKING AT YOSEMITE NATIONAL PARK

ABOUT THE AUTHOR

Kyle Spence was born in Dungannon, Northern Ireland and grew up around supermarkets. Since turning thirty he is slowly coming to terms with the fact that he might never again know the touch of a woman.

He thinks that he might like being a writer for Disney, but after two early novels of sex, violence and political incorrectness it's probably safe to say that this won't happen any time soon. But he is also willing to sell out (wink wink).

He is a lifetime member of the HP Lovecraft Historical Society, is a big fan of Frozen, Tangled and geeky stuff.

Merrily Merrily is his fourth novella and first venture into fantasy in a long time, unless you count daydreaming and procrastinating.

His latest novel Go Baby Go is a quirky sci-fi crime fiction about a Belfast thief working for the government of space on a job that keeps complicating itself.

He sincerely hopes that you have enjoyed this book, or at least paid for it because utility companies don't like it when he sends I.O.U.s.

Follow him online at wantonrambling.com

Also by Kyle Spence

All are available in print and ebook on Amazon

Novels

-Go Baby Go

Film Noir Love Story series
-Murder Incorporated
-Murder Syndicated

Novellas

-Two Days A Nightmare
-When the Man Comes Around
-The Music on the Lake
-Merrily Merrily

Printed in Great Britain
by Amazon

53163794R00108